P9-DHD-466

A Place Called Home

LORI WICK

HARVEST HOUSE PUBLISHERS
Eugene, Oregon 97402

Scripture quotations are taken from the King James Version of the Bible.

Except for certain well-established place names, all names of persons and places mentioned in this novel are fictional.

Cover by Terry Dugan Design, Minneapolis, Minnesota

About the Author

Lori Wick is one of the most versatile Christian fiction writers on the market today. From pioneer fiction to a series set in Victorian England to contemporary writing, Lori's books (over 1 million copies in print) are perennial favorites with readers. The Place Called Home series is a heartwarming saga of faith and love in the farmlands of Wisconsin. Born and raised in Santa Rosa, California, Lori met her husband, Bob, while in Bible college. They and their three children, Timothy, Matthew, and Abigail, make their home in Wisconsin.

A PLACE CALLED HOME

Copyright © 1990 by Harvest House Publishers
Eugene, Oregon 97402

Library of Congress Cataloging-in-Publication Data

Wick, Lori.
    A place called home / Lori Wick.
    ISBN 1-56507-588-9
    I.Title.
PS3573.I237P57   1990
813'.54—dc20   89-24445
                                                       CIP

All rights reserved. No portion of this book may be reproduced in any form without the written permission of the Publisher.

Printed in the United States of America.

· 99   00   01   02   /   BC   /   14   13   12   11

To Bob,
my husband and best friend
who never stopped believing
I could do this.

CAMERON FAMILY TREE

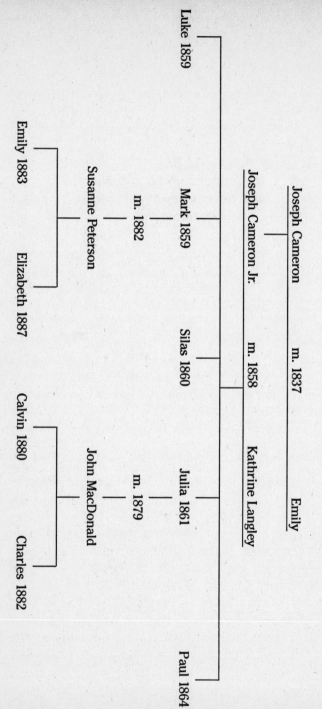

Joseph Cameron   m. 1837   Emily

Joseph Cameron Jr.   m. 1858   Kathrine Langley

Luke 1859

Mark 1859   m. 1882   Susanne Peterson

Emily 1883

Elizabeth 1887

Silas 1860

Julia 1861   m. 1879   John MacDonald

Calvin 1880

Charles 1882

Paul 1864

PROLOGUE

"...and to my coachman, Dobbins, I leave 300 dollars, the roan mare from the stables, and my black riding crop..."

The words became distant and far away to the black-garbed young woman, who sat as though she were made of stone. She sat in the large study that had been her grandfather's. This room had been his haven. It had been in this very room, on her grandfather's lap, that he had told her her parents were dead. They had drowned in a boating accident when she was six years old.

She used to love visiting her grandfather in this room. It was big and masculine, as he had been. Of course everything about Joshua Bennett had been big—his laughter, his temper, his love for life. She let her eyes wander around the room, whose walls were lined with books. She had learned to read and write in this room. Large, comfortable chairs were scattered about, and in the middle of it all was her grandfather's massive desk. The desk, the bookshelves, *everything* was walnut. The dark wood would have made it gloomy but for the two huge windows that sat behind the desk and overlooked the street. Her eyes went to the windows. It had begun to rain.

It was fitting that it should rain on the day of her grandfather's funeral and will-reading, since he never liked the rain. But her thoughts were brought abruptly back to the present at the mention of her name.

"...she will receive the house and stables along with the rest of my holdings. In the event of her death, the inheritance will go to my partner, Vince Jeffers."

Again the words of the lawyer faded from her ears. "In the event of her death everything will go to Vince Jeffers." Something is terribly wrong! Grandpa would never have done this! She tried to slow her racing thoughts as she brought her eyes to the man sitting not ten feet from her. Vince was watching her with a look that made her stomach turn. His too-thin face held a self-satisfied smile, making his long nose and dark eyes appear evil. It came to her at that moment that this man might in fact want every dime of her grandfather's money.

She rose and went to her room on legs barely able to support her. Once in her room, she sank into a chair and sat looking out at the pouring rain. Again the lawyer's words returned to her: "In the event of her death." My *death*? Grandpa would never write such a thing, since he was hardly leaving a fortune.

Her mind went back to her grandfather's study and the man who smiled so cynically at her. Fear welled up within her as she thought of her own death. With her grandfather gone, who would care? She didn't care about the money; all she wanted was her grandfather back. The tears she had held in until now streamed unchecked down her face. She had never felt so alone.

1

Mark Cameron paced the spacious entryway of his large, two-story house and looked at his watch for the fifth time. He walked to the foot of the stairs and called up, "Sue, are you almost ready? We're going to be late."

"I'll be right down," came the soft reply.

Mark resumed his pacing until the soft rustle of skirts sounded on the stairs. He turned just as his wife, Susanne, reached the bottom. His eyes lit with appreciation and he moved to take her hands in his. "Is Emily all settled in for the night?"

She answered as he helped her into her sweater, "She's cuddled into Maggie's lap with her favorite book and a blanket."

"And how is this little one down here?" Mark's hand moved down to rest tenderly on his wife's swollen abdomen.

Susanne laughed softly and covered her husband's hand with her own. "If he continues to move like he did today, he's going to make the next two months feel like a year."

Mark's thoughts went back nearly three years in time to the night Susanne had Emily. Mark was 25 and Susanne 23. He was a doctor and she a nurse, and both were experienced and confident. But their medical knowledge was little help that night with Susanne's long and hard labor. After Emily was born Susanne assured Mark it had been worth it all, and, looking at his beautiful baby daughter, he had to agree. Nevertheless, tonight his doubts began to surface and the concern he felt was evident in his voice. "Sue, are you sure you're up to this? If you're too tired, Mac and Julia will understand."

Susanne opened her mouth to reply, but someone pounding on the door stopped the words in her throat. Mark swung the door open quickly to reveal one of the boys from town trying desperately to catch his breath. Mark listened patiently as the boy spoke. Each word came out with a gasp. "Doc Cameron...a boy...in the alley...by the livery...stabbed...please hurry."

Mark turned to grab the black medical bag that was always kept in the entryway. He bent to give Susanne a quick kiss before moving out the door to follow the already-running boy. He heard his wife call "I'll pray!" as he broke into a run, hoping to cover the two blocks before it was too late.

Susanne closed the door and leaned against it. She took a moment to pray for Mark, the boy, and God's guidance this night. Removing her sweater, she walked up the stairs to tell Maggie the change in plans. Emily was nearly asleep. Once back in the entryway, she walked through a door that sat off to the right. Lighting lamps along her way, she entered her husband's office. She had no guarantee he would be bringing a patient tonight, but either way he would see the welcoming lights. She made sure the office door leading to the street was unlocked. Settling down to wait, she realized she must send word to Julia about supper.

Less than 20 minutes had passed when Mark came through the door with a limp bundle in his arms. He spoke quietly as he laid his burden down. "The cut isn't deep but he's lost quite a lot of blood. We need to get it stitched as quickly as possible."

Susanne picked up a cold, pale hand as her eyes moved over the boy. He was filthy from the top of his floppy hat to the boots on his feet (three sizes too large). His large pants and shirt were covered with a huge jacket, and the left shoulder of the shirt and jacket were stained with blood.

"I'll get his clothes, Mark, while you wash up."

As Mark entered the small equipment room, Maggie came through the entryway door. The two women moved silently and in one accord. First came the jacket. Moving the boy as little as possible, they cut the shirt away. Maggie pressed a cloth to the cut as it began to bleed again. The boy seemed to be wearing some kind of tight undershirt that Susanne cut off. As it fell away the women stared at each other across the body. Susanne moved first and reached for the hat. It was pulled on tight and took a bit of gentle tugging to break free. Again the women exchanged a long glance, before Susanne turned on her heel and walked into the equipment room.

Mark had dried his hands and was reaching for the tray holding all he needed to stitch the cut. Susanne stopped in front of him. "Is the boy ready for me?" He was met with silence.

Alarmed that something had happened, he moved to step around her, but Susanne caught his hand. He raised his eyebrows in surprise as Susanne replied, "Mark, your patient is not a boy—it's a young woman."

2

Mark Cameron's brothers Luke and Silas rode toward town. The warmth of the day, even at 7:00 A.M., told them August was going to be as hot as July. The men were headed to Mark and Susanne's. Luke was then to catch the 8:15 train for Chicago.

Things were still pretty quiet as they rode into town. They tied their horses in front of a large, white, two-story house that had served the town's medical needs for nearly 40 years. Joseph Cameron Sr. had converted the parlor into an office, and with great pride had turned it over to his grandson Mark upon completion of his medical training.

As the men walked to the front door, Luke's eyes went to his brother's work clothes. After Luke caught the train, Silas would be headed back out to the horse ranch they worked together, north of town. Luke was dressed in a suit that usually left the closet only for church. He envied Silas his comfort.

Susanne answered the door and each man hugged her. "We missed you last night at Julia's. Where's Mark?" Silas asked.

"He's upstairs with the patient who came in last night."

The fact that a patient was upstairs spoke of a serious injury. Each man knew better than to question Susanne. She was the soul of discretion, especially concerning Mark's practice.

She turned to the brother-in-law whose face mirrored her husband's. "Luke, will you take some things to Paul? It's not very much if you can fit them in your case."

"Sure, I'll work them in."

"Can you stay for breakfast?" Sue asked.

"I thought you would never ask!" Silas spoke as he moved toward the rear of the house. "Where's my niece?"

Susanne answered as she and Luke followed him. "She's supposed to be in the kitchen setting the table."

Emily was hard at work when the three entered the big, sunny kitchen. Her mother's voice broke through her concentration.

"Emily, your uncles are here." A big smile broke across the little girl's face, and with an excited squeal she moved around the table toward her uncles. Upon spying the way her Uncle Luke was dressed, she stopped in her tracks.

"Is this Sunday?"

"No," Silas answered.

Emily continued to frown in her Uncle Luke's direction until he came over and picked her up.

"How come you're dressed like Daddy today?" She, as well as the rest of the townsfolk, counted on the way the Cameron twins were dressed to tell them apart.

"I'm going on the train today."

"Will you be gone for my birthday?"

"I'm afraid so, but I'll bring you something from my trip."

Emily was more than pleased with his answer and was hugging him when her father joined them in the kitchen. Soon all five of them were seated at the table. Mark prayed, asking God's blessing upon the food, Luke's trip, and the patient upstairs.

After the prayer, Luke asked how serious the patient was.

"We're waiting out a fever right now."

"Is it someone we know?" Silas asked, concern in his voice.

"No, she's not from around here—at least I don't think she is." Mark's eyes went to his daughter and the conversation moved discreetly to Luke's trip. He would be gone about three weeks and planned to see Paul, the youngest of the Camerons, at the seminary he attended in Chicago. He was also to look into buying two mares and a stallion for the ranch.

The time moved quickly. Mark went back to work and his brothers were again on their horses and headed for the train station. Things were bustling at 8:00 and the platform was crowded as Luke bought his ticket.

The brothers talked as they waited for the train.

"You did get over to say goodbye to Grandma Em, didn't you?" Luke laughed at the question. "Let's put it this way, Silas: If I hadn't, I'd better not come back!"

Both men laughed and the train blew its whistle. They said their goodbyes and Luke moved along with the crowd to board. He settled into a seat and then waved out to Silas as the train pulled away. With the train gathering speed, he reached into his bag for the book he was reading and settled back for his trip to Illinois.

3

Christine Bennett fought against the blackness that threatened to engulf her once again. She was warm now but not burning up, as she had been before. Lying flat on her back on something soft, she knew without opening her eyes that it was daylight. She intended to lie there and try to organize her thoughts, but the sound of someone moving around the room was too much for her.

Peeking out between lids that rebelled at the idea, Christine focused slowly. She was more than a little surprised to find herself in a lovely bedroom that was not her own. Her eyes slowly took in the brightly flowered wallpaper and furniture, all painted white. The bed she was in was big enough for two of her, and sat off to the left side of the room. The far wall had a large window covered with white lace curtains, allowing the sun to stream in. Her eyes also took in a dresser, mirror, and rocking chair before coming to rest upon a woman bent over a plant in the corner.

The woman was dressed in a dark blue skirt and crisp white blouse. Her medium-brown hair was pulled back in a very businesslike bun. She hummed softly to herself as she watered.

Christine knew a moment of panic at not recognizing where she was; the thought made her squirm. The sound of her bedcovers moving brought an abrupt halt to the humming, and the woman advanced upon her with a beaming smile.

"Well, well, my dear. I had begun to wonder if you were ever going to wake up. My name is Margaret Pearson— 'Maggie' to my friends. Your fever broke during the night after nearly three days. I can tell you the Doc was glad of that! You've had us quite worried. It would have been a terrible thing to lose you, not even knowing your name. So tell me, my dear, what is your name?"

Christine looked into the face of this kind, smiling woman and realized she had never heard anyone speak quite so fast. Or maybe it was because she wasn't feeling herself.

Christine tried to speak, but the words came out in a croaked whisper. Maggie, immediately seeing the problem, drew Christine up with one arm and brought a glass of water to her lips.

Christine lay back and took a deep breath before attempting to speak again.

"My name is Chris—Christine Bennett. Please tell me whose house I'm in."

"Oh! Christine! What a lovely name. Makes me think of Christmas!" Maggie said with her beaming smile. "As to whose house this is, it's the doctor's house—Doc Cameron, his wife, and his little girl. This room is kept special for patients who need to stay over. I'm Doc Cameron's nurse. Well! Listen to me chatter! The Doc will want to know you're awake and I'm sure you must be starved." Maggie spoke over her shoulder as she headed for the door. "The Doc is a good man, the best doctor around these parts, but let me tell you, my dear, how fortunate you are. A few inches lower with that knife and the doctor would not have been able to help you."

Maggie then moved out the door and did not see the little color left in Christine's face drain away at the thought of her own death.

4

Christine lay looking at the ceiling as she listened to Maggie's footsteps recede down the hall. For a moment she had forgotten the alley, the man with a knife, and all the events leading up to her arrival in the small town of Baxter. She tried to shift around in the bed, but the movement brought a sharp pain to her shoulder. She decided to lie quietly, and as she settled in again she let her mind drift back to Spooner and the morning after her grandfather's funeral.

— ✛ —

"Christie, Christie dear, are you awake?"

"Yes, Mrs. Hall, come on in." The bedroom door opened and Mrs. Hall, Joshua Bennett's housekeeper of some 20 years, came over to the bed carrying a small serving tray. Christine pushed herself backward in her bed until she was propped up against the headboard. After setting the tray on the bedside table, Mrs. Hall sat on the edge of the bed and took Christine's hand in her own.

"How did you sleep, Christie?"

The gentle words brought tears that Christine thought she had cried out completely the night before. In an instant the women were both crying and in each other's arms. They clung tightly to each other in an attempt to soothe the hurt they were feeling and to fill the void hanging over them with the knowledge that Joshua Bennett was gone.

They separated after some minutes, each making an attempt to compose herself.

Mrs. Hall's smile was a bit shaky as she gestured to the tray. "I brought you some coffee and muffins."

Christine was not hungry, but as she looked at Mrs. Hall,

this precious woman who cared for her and the closest person she had had to a mother since she was six years old, she knew she couldn't hurt her.

"Thank you, Mrs. Hall." Christine tried a smile that was even more wobbly than Mrs. Hall's.

Mrs. Hall squeezed Christine's hand and shut the door as she left the room and Christine to her own thoughts.

Christine reached for the coffee and tried not to let her thoughts wander. She noticed that the rain had ended. It looked like a good day for a ride on Raven, her mare. She would need to sneak down the stairs and go out by way of the kitchen so her grandfather wouldn't catch her in the boy's pants she wore when she rode astride. Christine felt tears sting her eyes as she realized where her thoughts were headed. *Her grandfather was gone.* She decided against riding.

Knowing that if she stayed in bed she would continue to cry, Christine jumped up and began to dress. Her grandfather would not have wanted her depressed. She pushed her sad thoughts aside and was dressed and brushing her hair when another knock sounded at the door.

Opening the door revealed Mrs. Hall again. "Christie, Carl Maxwell was here and he—"

"Oh, Mrs. Hall, please tell him I'll be right down!" Christine interrupted as she turned back to the mirror to finish her hair.

Mrs. Hall followed her into the room. "Christie, he didn't stay." Christine stopped brushing and turned to look at Mrs. Hall. "I'm sorry, dear, but he simply asked me to give you this letter and said he had to be going."

Christine looked down at Mrs. Hall's extended hand. She had not even noticed the letter. Christine took the letter even as she wondered why Carl had not stayed for coffee, as was his usual practice. She dismissed the idea when she realized he was being polite in her time of grief. The truth of the matter was that she would have liked to talk with him.

So caught up was she in her own thoughts that she did not hear Mrs. Hall pick up the tray and leave as quietly as she had before.

Christine settled herself in a large, comfortable chair by the window and stared at the envelope. Christine's thoughts had wandered the night before over her grandfather's will and any involvement that Vince Jeffers might have had. Realizing what she was suspecting Vince of, she pushed all such ideas aside and opened the letter. She was not prepared for what she read.

Christie—

I'm sorry I could not stay to see you, but I had to let you know you are in danger. You must get away. Take the train to Fall Creek and stay there until I send for you. Tell no one where you are going and destroy this letter. When you get to Fall Creek go to the ticket office and find Mr. Franklin. Tell him I sent you. He will take care of you, see you settled, and keep in touch with me. I repeat, Christie, *tell no one*—just get out of the house tonight, and remember: You are in danger. Again, I'm sorry.

Carl

Christine sat frozen to the chair. She was in danger! Was Vince Jeffers involved? She read the letter again. He said to get out of the house tonight. She felt panic. She wasn't even sure where Fall Creek was. And who was this Mr. Franklin? She had to force down feelings of despair as she thought of leaving her home. With her grandfather gone, she didn't even feel she had a home. Thinking of her grandfather reminded her of how ashamed he would be if he saw her sitting there feeling sorry for herself. Her grandfather had trusted Carl Maxwell, and she would too. Her eyes went to the clock as she tried calmly to think of what she had to do and how much time she had to do it. Putting the letter in the pocket of her skirt, she prepared to go out.

At 11:20 P.M. Christine stood before the full-length mirror in her room and with a meticulous eye went over every inch of her appearance. Who would have thought the soberly dressed young woman who had walked sedately to the bank to withdraw money and then to the train station to check schedules could be standing here some hours later looking like the poorest beggar boy in town?

Her eyes started their survey with her boots. They were so big it was hard to walk, but they were all she could find. They must have been an old pair of the stable boys' boots because they looked a hundred years old. Her pants were so large they had to be held up with suspenders. The suspenders were also old, and one side kept coming undone. She had horrible visions of them coming loose as she boarded the train and causing a scene which the town would never forget when her pants dropped down around her ankles.

Her eyes traveled up to her shirt. The too-small camisole she had struggled into helped disguise most of her curves. The old jacket out of her grandfather's closet would finish the job. She blinked rapidly as tears came unbidden with thoughts of her grandfather. She had no time for tears.

Gathering the mass of red-brown curls that fell down her back, she held them atop her head. She jammed the floppy brown hat down hard. The hair made the hat too tight, but at least it would stay in place. Eyes back on the mirror, she reached for the small container of dirt she had dug from the garden. Her white face shone like a beacon under the dark brim of her hat. She powdered the dirt all over her face and down her neck. She also did the backs of her hands. Resisting the impulse to wash it off, Christine knew she would be safer traveling this way. She simply had no choice.

The clock now said 11:45 P.M. It was time to go, or she would miss her train leaving for Eau Claire at 12:45 A.M. She picked up her small bag (one of her grandfather's old cases with very little inside), blew out the light, and headed for the door.

Christine sat in the shadows of the train station waiting for the train to come in. She had her ticket and was trying desperately to stop trembling. She had gotten out of the house without a hitch and the walk to the train station had been no problem; she had been careful to stay away from the saloons. But the enormity of what she was doing was suddenly becoming real to her.

Hearing the train whistle, Christine's thoughts raced with all she was leaving behind. She hadn't even been able to say goodbye to Mrs. Hall. She blinked rapidly as tears threatened, but was under control before leaving her place in the shadows to board the train. No one paid any attention to her as she found her seat and sat staring out into the night. Glad for the cover of darkness as the train pulled out, the tears began to stream down her face. As the dim lights of the train station faded, she wondered if she would ever come home again.

— ✛ —

Most everything was quiet in Spooner as the train pulled away at nearly 1:00 in the morning. But on the other side of town a light could be seen shining in the den of one of Spooner's most prominent citizens.

"What took you so long?" The question was barked out in anger.

A scruffy little man stood in front of the big desk twisting his hat in his hands. The man behind the desk scowled impatiently. "I said what took you so long?"

"Well, sir, you said ta wait till all the lights was off."

"There were lights on upstairs at 11:30 at night?" the man behind the desk asked in angry disbelief.

"Well, yes, sir, but it's all dark now and everythin's quiet."

Still scowling, the man behind the desk asked, "Is everything ready for tomorrow night?"

"Yes, sir, me and the boys are all set. We'll be fast and quiet."

"See that you are." He bent over the papers on the desk, a gesture of dismissal for the little man.

"Uh, sir, about the fee..."

"You'll get your money when I see the body, and not a moment before. Is that understood?"

"Uh, yes, sir, yes, sir." The small man moved quickly toward the door, but stopped as the man at the desk spoke again. "Start keeping an eye on my new partner. Report back to me on his activities."

The man at the door nodded and moved on, only too happy to escape this big house and the man inside.

5

The rocking of the train was comforting as Christine sat looking out into the darkness. The busy day and late hour were catching up to her, and her eyelids drooped with fatigue. Before the train had covered five miles she was asleep.

When Christine awoke, it was daybreak and the train was pulling into Eau Claire. She was vaguely aware that a voice had called out stops along the way and she had dozed through them. She rubbed her eyes and snuggled her coat around her. She was completely unaware that her tears the night before, combined with the dirt she had powdered on her face, made her appear exactly as she had hoped—a tall, thin boy whose dirty appearance made him of no concern to anyone.

Hoping that none of her hair had slipped out, Christine carefully checked her hat with a small movement, so as not to draw attention to herself. She need not have worried. The hat was pulled on so tightly that it made her head ache!

She picked up her bag and moved into the aisle. The train station was crowded, but she made her way to the ticket window and was told the train to Fall Creek would be delayed. She took a seat further down the platform, being as inconspicuous as possible, and settled down to wait.

By the time her train was called, hours later, she was hot and thirsty and her bottom ached from sitting on the wooden bench. Seated again on the train, she took notice of the other passengers. There was a young woman with a baby, a very thin man with a fat wife, an elderly couple, and a businessman. All seemed to be wrapped up in their own thoughts, and Christine turned her gaze out the window. All of this countryside was new to her. She had been to Eau Claire with her grandfather on several business trips over the years, but never beyond.

She let her mind drift to Fall Creek. *Mr. Franklin.* Carl Maxwell had said to find Mr. Franklin and no one else. Would Mr. Franklin be able to answer some of her questions? Did he know what the danger was or if Vince Jeffers was involved? A chill ran up her spine at the thought of Vince Jeffers. So many unanswered questions. Why couldn't Carl have stayed and explained things to her? She reminded herself that her grandfather had trusted Carl Maxwell. Carl would not send her away unless he knew she would be cared for. Having reasoned this out, she closed her eyes and tried not to think anymore. A rumble in her stomach reminded her that she hadn't eaten today. Well, Fall Creek was the next stop. Hopefully Mr. Franklin would feed her.

"Fall Creek! This is Fall Creek, folks. Next stop is Rosedale. Leaving in 15 minutes. All out for Fall Creek." The conductor's voice sounded bored, as if he had said these words a thousand times before. But the words were far from boring to Christine's ears. At the mention of Fall Creek her heart began to pound and she was afraid her legs were not going to support her. Her hunger and tight hat forgotten, she moved along the near-empty platform toward the ticket window.

"Where to, son?" The man behind the window was looking at her with bored expectancy.

Being called "son" confused Christine into silence for a moment, and when she spoke her voice was stuttering and high-pitched. "Well, I, um, well, I'm looking for Mr. Franklin."

The man's eyes seemed to soften slightly. "Are you a relative or a friend of the family?"

"Uh, well, just a friend."

"Well, son, I'm real sorry, but you missed the funeral. It was this morning at 10:00."

"Funeral?"

The man didn't seem to notice her confusion. "Yes, son, as I said, I'm sorry it was so sudden. But if you go on up to the house, I know the family will welcome you. Nice folks, the Franklins. Why, I remember when my wife was sick, they brought us..."

But Christine didn't hear the words. Dead! Mr. Franklin was dead! Buried just today. The day she was coming to him for help. Was it her fault he was dead? Did someone kill him to try to get to her? If that were the case, then she had to get out of Fall Creek.

"All aboard!" the conductor yelled.

The train! She must get back on the train. She moved for the door and fell into a seat just as the train began to move. She stared blankly out the window. In a few minutes the conductor came by for her ticket. She paid him for the trip to Rosedale and again retreated behind her wall of misery.

She tortured herself with thoughts of a man named Mr. Franklin whom she never knew but might have died because of her. The finality of death weighed upon her as she thought of never seeing her grandfather again. Mrs. Hall, her home, and Vince Jeffers all crowded into her thoughts. Each time the conductor came by for her ticket she paid him to ride to the next stop. Unaware and uncaring of how many miles she had traveled, her mind was closed to everything around her.

"Reedsburg! This is Reedsburg, folks. Next stop is Baxter. All out for Reedsburg. Next town is Baxter."

Reedsburg! The fog began to clear as she said the word to herself. She remembered slowly that her grandfather had business dealings several years back with a man in Reedsburg. The man had wanted her grandfather to come down, but he was reluctant to travel the 200 miles in winter.

She was over 200 miles from home! She was getting off at the next stop, not caring where it was or if she knew anyone. She just had to get off this train before it took her any further from home. Her bag was in her hand and she was ready to go when the conductor called Baxter as the next stop. Christine was sure she had never heard of it before.

She was the only one to get off in Baxter, and her eyes

took in the small, near-empty platform. Her feet were on solid ground only a few minutes when she heard the conductor call "All Aboard!" She took a few steps away from the train and turned to watch it move down the tracks. There was a finality about it that scared her a little.

Turning back toward the train station, Christine noticed for the first time that evening was falling. Her eyes went to the sign posted on the side of the ticket office: Baxter, Population 396. She took a deep breath and remembered again how hungry and tired she was. Well, she was in Baxter for at least tonight. She set off for what appeared to be the downtown section of Baxter, intent on finding a place to stay and something to eat.

Back in Spooner, Mrs. Hall hurried to answer the knock at the front door. "Oh, Mr. Jeffers, it's you. I so hoped it would be the sheriff with some news."

Vince Jeffers spoke as he stepped inside. "What news, Mrs. Hall? What's happened?"

"Oh, haven't you heard? Christine is missing. She wasn't in her room this morning and no one has seen her since yesterday." The old woman wrung her hands and tears filled her eyes.

Mrs. Hall did not see the angry clenching of Vince Jeffers' jaw as he fought to regain control of his emotions. With effort his voice came out calmly. "You did the right thing in calling the sheriff, Mrs. Hall. I'll go around now and see him to offer my help. If he's heard anything I'll come back and tell you."

"Oh, thank you, Mr. Jeffers; I've been so worried."

The polite mask falling from his face, he nodded to the woman and stepped out into the evening. Standing with his fists clenched, he trembled with anger at this change in his plans. He stood for some minutes getting control of himself before stepping off the porch with a determined stride, a new plan already forming in his mind.

6

Christine moved around the back of the train station. There were barrels and crates stacked against the building. A lone wagon was parked nearby. There was little activity with the darkness coming, but as she came around the corner of the building she heard music playing. Looking across at what appeared to be a vacant lot, she decided to ask for help over there.

The backs of the other buildings she passed were as quiet as the train station had been. They had an ominous look, and she walked slowly and squinted into the darkness as she moved closer to the music.

As she arrived at the building it occurred to her for the first time that it was probably a saloon. She hesitated before starting up the alley toward the street and front door. Hating the thought of entering a saloon, she nevertheless had to find a place to stay for the night and a meal. She would have to swallow her fear and ask inside.

Halfway up the alley a voice spoke out of the shadows.

"Where you headed, boy?"

Christine gasped and backed away until she came up against the side of the building. A man then came out of the shadows. He didn't look very tall, but his upper body seemed massive in the dim light of the alley. If there was going to be a fight, there was little doubt in Christine's mind who would win.

"What's in your bag? A little cash, maybe?" His voice was deep and gravelly. "I've got me a thirst, boy, and no money. Maybe your bag there can help."

Christine moved the bag in front of her and grasped the handle with both hands.

"Now, listen boy, I don't want to hurt you. Just hand over the bag so I can see it."

Christine felt like a trapped animal. Her eyes searched for an escape route, but he was too close. Her eyes came back to the man who was slowly approaching her. The injustice of it all began to weigh upon her. The last 24 hours were crowding in. She was tired and hungry and her hat was too tight. Without the money in her bag she couldn't even get home. Home! At this point she could barely remember where that was.

The man was almost within arm's reach when he stopped and held out his hand. "Just give me the bag, boy, and you can be on your way."

"No!" Christine could hardly believe she had said that.

Before she could draw another breath the man moved. In an instant he held a large knife toward her. Christine's breath lodged in her throat.

"Now, boy, I'll say it one more time. Hand over the bag."

Christine acted before she thought. Still clutching the bag with both hands, she brought it up hard under the man's extended arm. His arm went up but he didn't lose the knife. Christine leaped away from him, but he was fast and she just barely missed being stabbed. Her fear turned to anger and new strength. She swung her bag again, but he grabbed it with his free hand. She saw him raise the knife and stood in stunned horror, knowing she was about to die. She heard a long, high-pitched scream, never realizing it was her own. She felt the bag wrenched away as a searing pain shot through her chest. She felt her knees buckle. Blackness engulfed her, and she knew no more.

Christine felt weary at having relived in her mind the events leading up to being in this room. Her weariness led to loneliness as she thought of how alone and far from home she was. What would become of her now?

Carrying a food tray, Maggie reentered the room at that moment. She reminded Christine so much of Mrs. Hall that tears flooded her eyes. Maggie set the food tray down and turned to smile at Christine with such tender understanding that, try as she might, she could not stem the flow of tears beginning to pour down her cheeks. Without a word, Maggie sat down and gently embraced the crying young woman. Wrapped in the loving arms of Maggie, Christine gave way to the healing tears that were to signal a change in her life that she could never have imagined.

7

When Christine awoke again it was to the pressure of a hand on her brow. The room was shadowed, dim, and easier on her eyes. She focused on the owner of the hand. A tall, handsome man with deep blue eyes was smiling at her.

"Welcome back. How do you feel?"

"Thirsty." Christine's voice was a hoarse whisper.

The man helped her drink and then settle back on the pillows before he spoke again.

"You were asleep each time I checked on you today. Maggie tells me your name is Christine Bennett." She nodded and he went on. "I'm Dr. Mark Cameron. I brought you here from the alley. What were you doing in the alley after dark?"

As he spoke, his hands were moving. He held her wrist for a minute and then checked her shoulder. He paused in his movements to meet her eyes, telling her plainly he was waiting for an answer.

"I was looking for something to eat and a place to stay for the night." She had been raised to tell the truth. She would not answer if it meant lying.

"You're not from Baxter?" He knew what her answer would be.

"No."

"Did you come in on the train?"

"Yes."

"You rode the train dressed as a boy?"

He watched her lips compress and an angry sparkle enter her eyes. He knew she was pulling away from him. He placed his hands gently on Christine's upper arms and said in a quiet but firm voice, "Christine, don't close me out. I realize you don't know me, but I want to help you if I can." He paused and watched her face intently for signs of softening. "Whatever it is that made you dress up like a boy and

28

leave your home is not going to go away just because you ran from it."

"You don't know how wrong you are!" she cried in a desperate voice. "I had to get out of Spooner."

Spooner! Mark carefully masked his surprise at how far she was from home. Then a thought came to him.

"Christine, you were stabbed in the alley. Was it someone you knew? Did you have something someone wanted?"

"I didn't know the man in the alley. He said he needed a drink and wanted my bag. He got it too—I mean, I think he did. You didn't find it in the alley, did you?"

"No, I'm afraid not."

She looked so young and vulnerable. Mark's heart went out to her. He decided to try one more time. "Talk to me, Christine. Let me help you."

To her utter horror and embarrassment her eyes filled with tears, and in an effort to keep from crying she began to talk. This man, stranger that he was, was so compassionate. She could not stem the flow of her words as the entire story came spilling out.

Outside of a question here and there, or a word of encouragement, Mark said nothing. His mind raced as he tried to sort through all the facts she was telling him. He agreed that she had no choice but to leave Spooner. He reassured her when she began to fret about the money in the bag, telling her everything was going to work out.

Once through talking, she was exhausted from the strain and terror of remembering. He helped her with another drink, this one mixed with a sedative she never noticed. She whispered a thank you as her eyes closed in sleep.

Not until Christine's breathing had evened out in deep sleep did Mark turn his attention to the third occupant of the room, whom Christine hadn't noticed. Susanne sat quietly near the door, where she had been during the entire exchange. Mark was sure the concern and sympathy he saw in his wife's eyes mirrored his own.

Having left Christine in Maggie's capable hands, Mark and Susanne checked on their own sleeping daughter and retired to the bedroom. As they prepared for bed, Susanne spoke for the first time. "I'm sure you realize she never intended to tell you a thing."

"I'm sure you're right." He paused and then added, "I can't help but think of Emily as a young woman, possibly alone. I would want someone to help her." His voice was heavy with despair.

"Oh, Mark, you know God would take care of her—just as I'm sure God put Christine in our lives because she needs us."

They were in bed now. Susanne lay on her side so Mark could rub the small of her back. She had done the wash today and ached all over. She was relaxed and near sleep when Mark spoke again.

"I'd like to see her up on her feet tomorrow, but I think she'll be embarrassed in front of me after tonight."

"You're probably right. Maggie and I can go in and get her up and dressed if she's ready for it."

"Since she is healing well, that will be fine. Thanks for handling it. Good night, Sue." He pulled her close and kissed her, and they both fell asleep with prayers in their hearts for Christine Bennett.

— ✧ —

Back in Spooner, once again in the ornate but dimly lit study, sat a man behind his desk in another late-night interview with the small, scruffy man who did his dirty work.

"Are you all set to get in tonight?"

"Yes, sir."

"Remember, if you get caught you're on your own."

"Me and the boys never get caught."

"Go alone!"

"What?"

"I said *go alone.* The three of you will wake the entire house if you search her room together. You go alone and quietly search through her clothes, drawers, everything. You mustn't leave a thing disturbed or that busybody Mrs. Hall will have the sheriff out again."

"Do you want I should get rid of her?"

"Of course not!" the man behind the desk snapped.

"Will that be all, Mr. Jeffers?"

"Yes, just as long as you continue to keep an eye on my partner and report to me regularly."

"Yes, sir, I'll do that."

"You may go, then."

As always, the little man was more than anxious to get away. He knew he wasn't much, but he didn't smile in a person's face and then pull a knife when his back was turned. Two-faced! There was no other way to describe Vince Jeffers, and he didn't trust him. Drawing deeply of the night air, he stepped out the rear of the house. The house, he thought, smelled evil, if that were possible. As he moved along in the shadows to do his night's work, he decided that when this entire episode with the Bennett girl was over he would take his share of the money and move on. He was getting too old for this type of work. His new resolve made him quicken his pace in an effort to get the job done and be gone.

8

Morning found Maggie, Susanne, and Christine all standing in Christine's room staring at each other. The two older women had entered the room and found Christine up, wrapped in a quilt, and looking out the window. Some minutes went by before Susanne broke the silence. She spoke as she transferred a bundle of clothes from her arms to the bed.

"I'm Susanne, Mark's wife." She paused, uncertain. This was not going at all as she had planned. "I brought you some clothes, but I don't think they're going to fit. I mean, you're welcome to them . . . they're mine, but . . ." She shrugged helplessly.

A smile broke across Christine's face at Susanne's attempt at tactfulness. She topped both of these women by a good six inches. Christine was still smiling when she spoke. "I appreciate your kindness and effort. It's hard to judge a person's height when she is in bed."

Both women returned her smile with great relief, and the tension in the room evaporated.

"Well, now," Maggie spoke in her no-nonsense way. "We'll have to look for something else while you get your bath and have breakfast. Maggie handed the clothes back to Susanne and stripped the bed. "Now, my dear, you sit back on the bed and I'll be back up in a minute with your bath." Both women moved out the door.

Christine was seated on the bed when Susanne stepped back into the room. "You must think me terribly rude, Christine. I didn't even ask how you felt."

Christine responded to the genuine concern she heard in Susanne's voice. "I'm a little stiff, but I guess that is to be expected." The women exchanged smiles and Susanne moved out the door again.

Christine knew a moment's embarrassment as Maggie assisted with washing her hair. The only person who had ever helped her was Mrs. Hall. But Maggie's efficient way soon had Christine at ease.

Christine had just finished breakfast and was seated on the edge of the bed, wrapped in a sheet, when Susanne returned. She handed Christine some undergarments.

"Put these on and I'll help you with your hair."

Christine opened her mouth to protest, but Susanne had already turned away to hang the dress and move the chair in front of the mirror.

Christine sat in silence, feeling a bit strange at having this woman, really a stranger, do her hair. But if the truth were known, her shoulder and arm were not up to it. So she was grateful.

Susanne worked in silence except for an occasional comment on how thick Christine's hair was or what a lovely color. Susanne would have laughed to know Christine was admiring the shining blonde curls on her own head with a bit of envy. As Susanne moved to Christine's side, Christine's eyes fell to her swollen stomach. She had made an effort not to stare, but she had been around so few women with babies that she was fascinated. Her cheeks burned as she raised her eyes and met Susanne's, knowing she had been caught staring.

"Do you like children?" Susanne asked quietly.

"Yes." The reply was just as quiet.

The only sound for a time was that of the brush moving through Christine's hair.

"Maggie may have told you that this is our second child. We have a little girl, Emily, who is with her Grandma Em today. Mark has never said, but I'm sure he hopes for a boy. I guess most men want a son. But either way we'll love and cherish this one too. Children are a special gift from the Lord."

Christine was quiet for awhile, digesting Susanne's last statement. Susanne left her to her thoughts.

"How old is Emily?"

"She'll be four before the baby is born."

"When is the baby due?"

"About seven weeks," Susanne answered as she set the brush down. "But at this point it feels like seven years."

Susanne turned and brought the dress over for Christine. "Here, try this for size."

It was a beautiful dress, plum-colored with small white flowers running through it. Christine looked down at herself and then in the mirror. It wasn't too short in the sleeves or the hem, and she was amazed. Her feelings must have shown because Susanne laughed and said, "Mark has a sister about your height."

The words were sobering for Christine, her pride reminding her that she did not even have money for clothes. The thought saddened her. Susanne didn't seem to notice. "Put your shoes on and I'll show you the house."

Susanne led the way out and next door to Emily's room. All thoughts of sadness disappeared at the sight of this little girl's room. Everything was in pinks, delightfully feminine. Frilly curtains and bed ruffle perfectly matched a flowered quilt and wallpaper. In one corner was a doll's cradle with several doll babies sleeping peacefully. In another corner stood a tiny rocking horse, and a stack of books was resting neatly.

Susanne then led the way to the master bedroom across the landing from Emily's room. It was larger, with windows on two walls, and was dominated by a huge bed. Christine's eyes went briefly to Susanne's petite frame and thought she must feel lost in it. She had decorated the room in warm brown tones with a touch of rust and tan. Beautiful lace doilies donned the tables flanking the bed. Bookshelves near the windows were filled. Christine assumed they were medical journals. The room was warm and bright. Christine praised Susanne's decorating style.

The last bedroom upstairs was the baby's, the smallest

of the four bedrooms and perfect for the expected infant. The cradle was filled with quilts and the walls were painted a soft yellow. Susanne opened a chest under the window and brought out a few tiny nightclothes. Christine fingered the soft material, thinking of the two women she had known with babies. They really had been more acquaintances than friends.

Descending the stairs put them in the entry by the front door. To one side of the entryway Susanne showed her a door, explaining that at one time it had been the parlor but was now Mark's office.

Opposite the office door and right off the entryway was the front door, but Susanne led them down a back hall that ran along the stairs and took them to the kitchen.

The kitchen was bright and perky. The cupboards were painted white and appeared spotless. There was an alcove holding a table and four chairs. The curtains, tablecloth, and fabric covering the pantry shelves were all red gingham. Another door, Susanne said, opened to Maggie's bedroom. The massive stove and oven were shiny and clean, making Christine think that Susanne certainly had enough to keep her busy.

Christine followed Susanne from the kitchen to the dining room. All along one wall was a beautiful built-in sideboard and glass-fronted cupboards with lovely glassware and dishes. They walked past the dining table and chairs into the front room.

The front room had a lived-in elegance about it. The couch and chairs were all covered in varying shades of blue, and all sat on a beautiful cream-colored rug. An upright piano sat near the stairs, music opened, looking ready to be played. The piano, bookshelves, and tables were all in a dark wood.

When Susanne stopped, Christine told her how lovely she found the home. Susanne smiled in her quiet way and suggested that Christine sit and rest a bit before lunch.

More tired than she cared to admit, Christine simply thanked her and took a chair by the window. Susanne took her leave to the kitchen and Christine turned her attention to the street.

9

Christine noticed that things were fairly quiet out on the street. She noted that houses across the street were nicely painted and maintained. She watched two little boys walk by, and then a woman with a large basket. Christine sat absorbed with the activity in the street until she heard light footsteps on the carpet. Turning, she found a beautiful little blonde girl regarding her with big blue eyes.

Christine smiled and said, "You must be Emily."

Emily nodded.

"My name is Christine."

"Why are you wearing my Aunt Julia's dress?"

The question took Christine by surprise. "Well, I didn't have a dress to wear and your aunt was kind enough to let me borrow hers."

"Where are your dresses?"

Unaccustomed to speaking with children, Christine was not quite sure how to answer. She opted for honesty. "I left my home in a hurry and my dresses were left behind."

"Will you buy some here?"

"Well, not right now, not until I have some money." (As Christine had been gazing out the window, she had decided to find work as soon as possible.)

"But if you have no money, how will you pay my daddy for making you all better?"

"Emily!" A deep, masculine voice spoke sharply from the edge of the room. Emily spun around to face her father, her small hand going to her mouth as she realized who had heard her.

Mark advanced slowly and spoke quietly to Emily when he stopped before her. "You will apologize immediately and then you will go to the kitchen and help your mother with lunch." Emily turned slowly back to Christine and spoke quietly. "I'm sorry, very much."

Christine reached out a hand and gently touched the top of Emily's shiny blonde head. Unsure of what to say, she simply smiled her kindest smile so Emily would know all was forgiven.

Emily smiled back with a hesitant look at her father to see if she had done all right. His nod was her reward, and she walked quickly from the room.

Mark took a chair near Christine, intending to make his own apologies, but Christine spoke first.

"Emily is right, you know. I haven't a dime to my name. I was, as a matter of fact, just sitting here thinking about a place to live and a job, hoping there would be something right here in town." She smiled a small smile. "I really feel I have traveled enough for the time being."

Mark listened to her speak. As he had half expected, she was calm, self-assured, proud. Gone was the crying girl from last night. She did not take easily to a handout, he was sure of that. She was in a fix and planned to work her way out. Mark could easily pay her way home, but he felt this morning that God was leading him to keep her near for the moment. Christine's own words confirmed this thought. "I thought you might feel that way, Christine. Why don't I tell you of an idea I have during lunch?"

"Oh, thank you, Dr. Cameron, that's very kind of you," Christine replied as she stood and moved toward the kitchen. She turned back to say she was going to lend a hand with lunch, but Mark stood also and Christine found herself staring speechlessly into his chin. Mark watched her eyes drop to his shoes and then her head tilt back as her eyes met his. He had to fight to keep from laughing as he watched her mouth drop open. She stared this way for some moments before Mark spoke.

"My sister Julia is your height. Outside of her husband and her brothers, there are not many men she has to look up to. From the look on your face, it must be the same for you." His voice was full of amusement and Christine's mouth shut with a snap. Her cheeks flamed with embarrassment as she realized how she had been staring, her mouth hanging open like a codfish on a hook.

Not knowing what to say, she mumbled something about helping with lunch and made a hasty exit, thinking as she did so that Baxter had held more embarrassing moments in less than a week's time than Spooner had in 19 years!

Lunch went fine, Mark felt, as he walked toward his grandmother's house. Christine had been very receptive to his job idea. She was a sweet young woman who seemed to get along well with everyone. Now if he could convince Grandma Em that she and Christine needed each other, everything would be fine. He found himself wishing Luke were here. Luke had a certain way with Grandma Em. Maybe he would try a bit of Luke's firmness with her if it came to that.

He knocked on the front door and entered. "Hello, anyone home?" His footsteps echoed loudly on the polished wood floor of the parlor before hitting the rug. He passed through the parlor and into the kitchen, spying his grandmother through a window as he walked. She was out by her flower garden in the backyard. Her neighbor, Mr. Turley, was by her side. After kissing his grandmother, he turned to shake Mr. Turley's hand.

"Hello, Mr. Turley, how are you today?"

"Well, I'll tell you, Mark, if I were any better I wouldn't be able to stand myself."

Mark laughed and Mr. Turley spoke again.

"I saw that little Emmy of yours this morning." Emmy was his name for both the old and young Emily Camerons. "You've got yourself a real gem there."

"Thank you, Mr. Turley. We think she's pretty special."

"Well, Emmy, I've got work to do. I'll see you later. You too, Mark." He turned to go home.

"So, what brings my favorite grandson over?" Mark smiled at his grandmother's familiar line.

"I'm here on business today."

"Sounds serious. I best put on a pot of coffee."

Mark walked back to the house at his grandmother's side and then watched her move around the kitchen preparing coffee and setting out cookies. He prayed again about her response to his idea. She could be very stubborn if she chose to be. For an instant he thought about the sparks that might fly if he put these two strong-willed women together. If his guess about Christine was right, she was more than a little independent.

The tinkling sound of china cups broke into his thoughts as Grandma Em brought a tray laden with coffee, cups, and cookies to the table.

They poured their coffee in silence. When Mark felt his grandmother watching him, he looked up and met her eyes squarely.

"I'll start by telling you we have a young woman staying with us."

"Emily said there was a sick lady in the room next to hers and you were going to make her all better."

Mark smiled at his daughter's vote of confidence. "Her name is Christine Bennett, and healthwise she's doing fine. But there has been some trouble involving her, and I'm afraid I can't share it with you. I will tell you that she's not from around here and she has no one to call on for help. Christine told me she wants to find work. I could offer to pay her way home, but I'm sure I would be turned down. I doubt Christine takes kindly to a handout."

Mark took a breath and decided to jump in with both feet. "I'd like her to come and work for you."

Emily Cameron stiffened and opened her mouth to tell her grandson exactly what she thought of the idea, but his raised hand stopped the words in her throat.

"You will hear me out." His voice was so stern and commanding she could do nothing but comply.

Over an hour later Mark was walking back to his office. Grandma Em had balked at the idea of a strange young woman coming not only to work for her but to live with her as well. Mark reminded her of hauling wood in November when her arthritis was giving her fits, of going out in the snow to feed the handful of livestock she stubbornly refused to sell, of a horse that was older than Mark was, of a useless goat who needed his vocal chords removed, of four laying hens now too tough to eat, and of two huge white pigs.

Before the conversation ended she had admitted she was feeling a bit tired. Grandma Em even went so far as to confess that when she had dusted the parlor yesterday, she had knocked the portrait of the grandchildren onto the floor and shattered the glass. She had then put the picture away in the closet until she could order more glass.

As Mark entered his office, he felt sure the job would work out between the two. Christine, having lived with her grandfather, would certainly know how to be helpful in a tactful way.

10

Two days later Mark walked beside a silent Christine toward his grandmother's house. He carried a small case belonging to Susanne that held the dresses and such that Julia had sent over for Christine. Mark looked down at Christine's face and saw a mixture of determination and fear. He was on the verge of reassuring her when she spoke.

"Did you talk to the sheriff about my being stabbed?"

"Yes, and I also told him briefly of your situation." Christine looked troubled at this, so Mark spoke again. "He had to know, Christine. If there should be any stranger asking around, the sheriff would need to know why."

"But no one knows I'm in Baxter."

"That's true, but the fact still remains that someone did stab you, and although the sheriff agreed with me that it was probably not related to your home situation, there is no reason we should take chances."

The feelings of safety which Christine had harbored at being so far from Spooner and Vince Jeffers now evaporated. But Mark and Christine were already walking up the wide steps to the large porch and front door of Grandma Em's house. The fact that this house was going to be Christine's new home for an indefinite period of time banished all other thoughts from her mind.

Christine followed Mark into a lovely parlor and sat as he directed. Mark disappeared but returned shortly, preceded by a woman of medium height whose steps belied her 70 years. Her hair was a silvery white and in close curls around her head. Her face was liberally seamed and the expression in her light blue eyes was hesitant. It occurred to Christine at this moment the woman was not very happy about the idea of her working here. This thought put Christine on the defensive, and her eyes went to Mark's face.

After Grandma Em had seated herself across from Christine, Mark made introductions. "Gram, this is Christine Bennett. Christine, this is Emily Cameron—"Grandma Em" to her friends, old and new alike."

The women exchanged hesitant smiles and nods. Each measured the other with different thoughts flying through her head.

Emily knew she was fighting God's will as she sat there hating herself for getting old and hoping to find something about this girl she didn't like to ease her conscience when she told Mark that it would not work out. She feared this girl would come in and take over. Life as she had always known it would be changed forever and she had always struggled with change.

Christine, with her own thoughts, wondered if this woman was kind or unreasonably set in her ways—ways that did not include another woman in the house. Needing this job desperately if she were going to get her life back in control, Christine decided to be sweet and congenial.

Grandma Em broke the silence. "How old are you, Christine?"

"Nineteen, ma'am."

"And you're familiar with work around the home and yard?"

"Yes, ma'am. Mrs. Hall, my grandfather's housekeeper, taught me everything she knew about running a home."

"Well, you understand, of course, that I will be running *this* house and you would be helping me." Emily's voice was sharper than she had intended.

Christine only nodded, afraid to say more lest it be the wrong thing.

"Have you ever stolen anything?" Emily asked abruptly.

All ideas of sweetness and congeniality flew out the window. Christine stood up so quickly that the chair nearly tipped over. Her eyes flashing with anger and pain, she turned accusingly to Mark. "I don't have to sit here and take this. How dare she ask me such a thing!" Too upset to say more, she turned and nearly ran out of the room. Mark caught her at the front door.

Emily sat frozen in the front room, her hand pressed tightly to her mouth, listening to the furious whispers at the front door. She prayed fervently that Mark would bring Christine back so she could ask her forgiveness. Why had she said such a thing? A woman her age should be beyond such foolishness.

Mark escorted a sober-faced Christine back to her chair, eyes wide and suspiciously wet. Mark sat near his grandmother, knowing she would do the right thing.

"Christine," Emily hesitated, but Christine caught the different tone in her voice—gentle, subdued. "Christine, please forgive me. I don't know why I said such a thing." Again she hesitated. "Well, the truth is, I *do* know. I didn't want it to work between us. You see, I'm old and set in my ways and very afraid of change. Mark tells me you're alone, and I think maybe we need each other." Emily's voice became quieter as she spoke, showing Christine that in this area she was as vulnerable as she was. Emily's voice was just above a whisper when she asked, "Will you stay, Christine?" This woman's honesty went straight to Christine's heart. She felt a sting behind her eyes and a tightness in her throat, enabling her to only nod and smile.

Mark's laugh of relief brought all three to their feet. He hugged Grandma Em and then surprised Christine by hugging her also. She had also felt surprised that morning when, after thanking Susanne and Maggie for everything, they had grabbed her and hugged her too. Spontaneous displays of affection were foreign to Christine, but she was beginning to like it.

Mark took his leave after Grandma Em served coffee. The two women spent the remainder of the day working in the garden, sharing companionable conversation, listening and learning with no doubt in either heart that they had found something special.

Christine snuggled down into the covers of the big oak bed. Her bed! The thought felt wonderful. She realized as she lay there that she and Grandma Em had spent so much time outdoors that the only rooms she had really seen were the parlor and kitchen and her own room. Her own bedroom! A feeling of contentment washed over her. Drifting off to sleep with her mind becoming foggy, she would have been hard-pressed to tell you if she had a single care in the world.

— ✛ —

"Are you sure no one saw you?"

"No, Mr. Jeffers, no one saw me."

"You went alone?"

"Yes, sir."

"Where did you say you found this?" Vince Jeffers held out a small piece of paper.

"In the closet, in the pocket of a skirt."

"Did you read it?"

"No, sir, I never learned." The small man stared at the carpet as he mumbled this. He looked up as he heard paper rustling and found Vince Jeffers reading the note. He watched as the man's jaw clenched and then threw the paper to the desk.

"The note is from Carl Maxwell." The small man's eyes widened at this information. "He told her to go to a friend of his in Fall Creek—a Mr. Franklin, it says." Vince Jeffers' voice became very calm as he continued. "Let's call around and visit Carl Maxwell, shall we? We'll ask him about this Mr. Franklin in Fall Creek. It's nearly midnight, but I'm sure we can convince him to talk with us."

The small man followed as Vince led the way out of the room. Once outside Vince spoke again, softly and more to himself than to the man behind him.

"Fall Creek. I wonder why he sent her to Fall Creek. Well,

it doesn't matter. Even if she's not there, wherever she is I'll find her, and when I do"—he paused, a cold smile playing over his thin lips—"when I do, everything will be mine."

11

At 9:30 A.M. Mrs Hall opened the door to admit the sheriff.

"Thank you for coming so soon. I just had to see you." Mrs. Hall's voice was anxious.

"Of course, Mrs. Hall. The stable boy said you had news."

"Yes. Well, you see, I remembered the day before Christine disappeared"—Mrs. Hall's voice shook and she stopped to take a breath. "The day before Christine disappeared, Carl Maxwell was here. He didn't stay to see Christine, but he left a note for her. I delivered it to her myself."

"Did you read the note?"

"No, of course not." Mrs. Hall's voice was indignant.

"Do you have the note now?"

"Well, no. When I remembered this morning, I went up and looked in her room but found nothing."

"I'll have a look myself." The sheriff moved toward the stairs and Mrs. Hall followed. "Describe this note to me—size, color..."

Less than an hour later Mrs. Hall was seeing the sheriff to the door. "I'm going to see Carl Maxwell. Hopefully he'll be able to explain the note."

"Maybe she took it with her." Mrs. Hall suggested.

"That's possible."

"Please, sheriff, please keep me informed. My little Christie is out there, away from home. She's never been away from home, and I fear she needs me." The sheriff watched the old woman's eyes fill with tears. He patted her shoulder awkwardly before moving away with a frown on his face, wishing with all his heart he knew where Christine Bennett was.

— ✥ —

Sunshine crept over the windowsill and into Christine's eyes, waking her into confusion. This was not her bedroom at home, or at Doc Cameron's. Where was she? Grandma Em's! The thought brought her instantly awake. Sitting upright in bed, a smile played across her sleep-flushed face.

She sat and surveyed her room from the bed. A soft blend of greens and peaches greeted her eyes. Everything had looked much darker in the lamplight the night before. The greens ranged from a very dark green rug to a pastel green ruffle around the bed. The wallpaper was in peach and yellow flowers with lots of green leaves and vines. The round table by the bed was covered in the same fabric as the bed ruffle. Lacy curtains in soft peach allowed the sunlight to flood in. In one corner was an oak desk and chair. Opposite the desk was a built-in closet. Below the window sat a low oak chest. Christine sat on it and looked out into the garden that Grandma Em had tended yesterday. Further back was a small barn, the sight of which reminded Christine that she would "meet" the animals today.

Having washed, dressed, and descended the stairs, Christine stood in the parlor, where she had met Grandma Em yesterday. Christine noticed for the first time the very ornate and beautifully carved pieces of furniture. The tables and legs of each chair were all intricately carved and matched.

"The furniture was my mother's." Emily's voice came from the kitchen doorway.

"It's beautiful."

"The chairs and sofa have been recovered." She ran her hand over a chair upholstered in a deep burgundy velvet. Curtains in the same material made things a bit dark for Christine's taste, but lovely nonetheless.

"After my father died, Joseph, my late husband and I, lived with my mother. We moved to Baxter from New York when Joseph Jr.—that was Mark's father—was ten. My mother decided to move in with her sister and gave us most of her furniture. The oak bed in your room was mine as a little girl. Well, we had best get to the barn. If you would let me, I'd reminisce all day."

Once they were in the barn, Christine watched Grandma Em fork hay to a horse who looked too old to be standing. His back swayed to an impossible depth and his nose was as gray as hoarfrost. However, his eyes looked gentle, and he turned like an old friend at the sound of Emily's voice. His name was Caesar.

The quiet bleating that had begun when Grandma Em and Christine entered the barn raised to a sound of desperation by the time Caesar was fed. Chester, Christine was informed, did not like to be kept waiting. Chester turned out to be a goat. He, like Caesar, looked old, but there was certainly nothing wrong with his voice. Christine's eyes widened in surprise at how fast the noise stopped as Grandma Em poured a scoop of grain before him.

Christine was still staring at the silent goat when Grandma Em threw a handful of corn to the hens and moved to sit on a bench near the door. Grandma Em pulled on an old pair of men's work boots, picked up a large pail, and beckoned to Christine to follow her out the door.

Christine caught up with her just as she stopped in front of a pen holding two of the biggest pigs Christine had ever seen. Christine's mouth dropped open in surprise as Grandma Em opened the gate, picked up her skirts, and entered the pen. The pigs ignored the open gate. Pushing and grunting with obvious delight at seeing her, they rushed toward Grandma Em. She laughed and spoke to them in quiet tones as she tipped the pail into their trough.

Emily then made her way back out to Christine and laughed at the look of disbelief on her lovely face.

"My grandchildren feel just as you do about Belle and Betsy. They are forever after me to sell all my animals. They just don't realize how attached I've become." Emily patted

Christine's arm. "Don't worry, dear, the animals will get used to you and love it when you feed them."

Emily turned away then and did not see the fresh look of dismay that crossed Christine's face. Christine shook her head in disbelief at what she had gotten herself into.

The women worked well together. They prepared and ate a quiet breakfast. Christine rose afterward, intending to clean up the dishes, but Grandma Em waved her back to her seat. "This is part of my morning routine, Christine." Christine watched her reach for a large black Bible. She opened the book and began to read aloud, giving Christine no time to be embarrassed or to comment.

" 'Give ear to my words, O Lord; consider my meditation. Hearken unto the voice of my cry, my King and my God, for unto thee will I pray. My voice shalt thou hear in the morning, O Lord; in the morning will I direct my prayer unto thee, and will look up.' Psalm 5:1-3."

Grandma Em closed the book and bowed her head. "Dear heavenly Father, I praise and thank You for the beautiful day You have given us and the blessings You daily give us. May we be mindful of You and ever in Your service." Grandma Em continued to pray, but Christine opened her eyes to see if anyone else was in the room. The only people she had ever heard pray were the preachers at her parents' funeral and later at her grandfather's. But neither one had sounded like this. Grandma Em made it so personal, as though God were right in the room with them. With another quick look around, Christine closed her eyes again. "And Father, I thank You for Christine. She is already so precious to me. Having her here has brought added sunshine to my life. Please bless and keep her and give us a special day together. In Christ's name I pray, Amen."

Christine, having never had a person pray for her, did not know what to say. To her surprise, no words were necessary. Speaking as if nothing were out of the ordinary, Grandma Em reached for the coffeepot and told Christine what she wanted to do that day. Quickly doing the dishes so they could walk to town before it got too hot, Christine wondered again about Grandma Em and the other people she had met in Baxter. They were not like any people she had known before.

On the walk to town, Grandma Em and Christine's conversation moved to family.

Christine asked, "Grandma Em, you talk as though Dr. Mark's father was dead. Is his mother alive?"

"No, she died when Paul—that's Mark's youngest brother—was only nine."

"How many brothers does Dr. Mark have?"

"Three—Luke, Silas, and Paul—plus one sister who is married and has two little boys of her own. Paul is at school in Chicago and Luke is there on a buying trip. You'll meet everyone else on Sunday, when we all go to church together and then back to my house for dinner."

Grandma Em stopped walking and turned abruptly to face Christine. "Christine, it hadn't occurred to me to ask you if you wanted to go to church with us. I just assumed you would. You will come with us, won't you?" Grandma Em's face was anxious.

Christine could see this was important to Grandma Em. She wouldn't think of refusing her. It gave her a warm feeling to be included as though she were a member of the family. Her answer was simple: "I'd love to come."

Christine found herself being hugged then, although she never found out why. Afterward Grandma Em hooked her arm through Christine's and they continued toward town, a brilliant smile lighting Grandma Em's face.

They stopped at the post office and then the general store. People greeted them warmly, and when the situation afforded, Christine was introduced. They found out that Lars Larson, who was going to paint Grandma Em's porch and shutters, had broken his arm. Emily brought it up on the walk home.

"Well, I'm sorry Lars broke his arm, but I'm also sorry that my painting probably won't get done before winter."

"Why don't we do the painting ourselves?"

Grandma Em stopped and looked at Christine as though she had never seen her before.

Christine continued, "I could climb the ladder and you could work below. We could do it after we do the canning this next week, or we could start right away."

"Luke would be angry," Emily said in a quiet voice, but Christine could tell she was thinking.

"You said Luke was in Chicago," Christine reminded her with a mischievous light in her sparkling green eyes.

Emily bit her lower lip in an effort to keep from laughing, but she couldn't hold it in. "We'll do it!" she said in a burst of laughter. "We'll start right away on Monday and then do our canning the next week." Grandma Em talked a bit more about the painting and then the women walked in silence for awhile. When the silence was broken, it was Emily asking Christine a question.

"Christine, someone is bound to ask me where you're from or why you're in Baxter. I have no wish to pry or to embarrass you, but, maybe you could give me a little help." Emily stopped talking then, praying she hadn't said too much. If she drove this young woman away, she would never forgive herself.

Christine's answer was long in coming, and her voice was quiet and hesitant. "My grandfather died about two weeks ago. We lived up north. I was on my way south to stay with someone.... When that didn't work out, I stayed on the train and found myself in Baxter. Upon arriving, my bag was stolen and I was attacked. That's how I met Dr. Mark. Losing my bag made work necessary." They had continued to walk as Christine spoke and were now home and seated on the front porch.

"But even if I hadn't been hurt, I would have stayed and rested for awhile before starting home."

"Thank you for sharing with me, Christine. I'll be praying for God's special comfort over your loss." Emily stood and put a comforting hand on Christine's shoulder. "Please remember, Christine, I'm here for you. If there is anyone at home you want to contact, feel free to use the paper and stamps in the desk in your room."

Emily left Christine alone on the porch. She was glad she had asked. Christine had been honest with her, of that she was sure, but neither had she told the entire story. Emily's mind went back to her meeting with the sheriff in the general store that morning. When Christine had been across the store looking at bolts of fabric, the sheriff had approached her and asked outright if the young dark-haired woman was Christine Bennett. Emily had been a little surprised when he had done nothing more than thank her and walk away after she had told him yes.

Emily climbed the stairs to her room. A pensive look on her face, she prayed that God would give her the needed wisdom to help this girl she was sure He had placed in her life.

Christine was not long in following Grandma Em indoors. Going to her own room, she sat at the desk. As she sat there she realized she had been trying to block Spooner and its problems from her mind. And for awhile it had worked. The paper was in the desk, just as Grandma Em had said. She toyed with it a moment before pulling some out. Determination on her face, she began to write. Even if it meant confronting Vince Jeffers herself, she wanted some answers!

Christine could not have known that a small, nondescript man was boarding the train in Spooner. His destination: Fall Creek. His purpose: to do Vince Jeffers' bidding.

12

Sunday dawned warm and lovely, but the beauty of the day was lost on Christine. Staring at her reflection in the full-length mirror which hung on the inside of her closet door, her thoughts were more suited to rain.

The dress she wore was mint green, lightweight, and fresh-looking. With short puffed sleeves, a fitted bodice, and a full skirt, the dress was really quite lovely and looked as though it had been made for her. A frown clouded her face as she remembered it hadn't been. Continuing to frown into the mirror, she realized how important it had become that Grandma Em's family and friends like her. Being out of her element and dependent upon other people brought a rush of insecurity to Christine.

As Christine descended the stairs she decided to relax and be herself. Her lack of close friends in Spooner had been because of where she lived, not because people didn't like her. Joseph Bennett's neighbors had been elderly, which probably explained why Christine had grown close to Grandma Em so quickly.

Being busy helped Christine get her mind off her troubles, so with a determined step she headed to the kitchen to start breakfast. Turning from her work, she heard Grandma Em's footsteps approach.

"Good morning, Christine. Oh! You look lovely, and your hair up like that is darling!"

"Thank you." Christine's raised hand to her hair showed Grandma Em how unsure she had been.

"Oh, Christine, there will be three of us for breakfast. Silas and Luke always take care of the stock on Sundays and then take us to church."

Christine noted that Grandma Em talked to her as though she had been a part of the family for years. Emily headed off in the direction of the dining room, counting aloud the number of family expected for lunch.

Christine continued with breakfast preparations when the door leading to the backyard burst open. In strode a man, who without a glance in Christine's direction went to the washstand. Christine stood still, her eyes taking in dark hair and a full, dark beard. His shirt tightened across a broad back and muscular arms as he reached for the soap. His height made him a Cameron.

As he washed, and without looking up, he began to speak in an exasperated voice. "Gram, those pigs are a nuisance. How you stand it is beyond me! And that goat! I was ready to nail his mouth shut this morning. Plus I made the mistake of going out to the pigs before giving corn to the chickens. They followed me and kept up a steady stream of chatter the whole time I was wading in to feed those two monstrosities you call pigs."

Silas Cameron turned from his washing to see he was not addressing his grandmother. He did not know this woman who stared at him as if he had lost his mind, but he was warm to his subject, so he continued. With little more than a flicker of surprise showing in his deep blue eyes (eyes that must be a Cameron trait, Christine thought), he went on.

"Have you seen those pigs?" he asked her directly.

"Belle and Betsy?"

"Right. Well, I'll tell you this family could be eating ham and bacon for years if she'd let us butcher those two. Everyone tried to tell her when she and Grandpa bought this place, but no, she said she felt sorry for the animals and Grandpa never could tell her no. So here we are, how many years later still taking care of—" He stopped when he saw his grandmother standing in the doorway, an amused smile playing across her lips.

Silas was always much quieter than his brothers and sister. He was not one you interrupted—for fear of shutting him up, never to know when he would start again.

Emily now openly smiled at her grandson. Silas returned the smile as he moved over to bend and kiss her cheek. Straightening, he leveled a look at Christine.

"Gram, introduce me to this poor girl who was forced to stand here and listen to me rant and rave."

After the introduction, and while he was still warm to the subject, Silas shot another question at Christine.

"What do *you* think of Belle and Betsy?"

"Well, they do grow on you."

Christine watched him throw back his head and roar with laughter, giving her a glimpse of beautiful white teeth amid his bearded face. His eyes were still sparkling with mirth when he said, "Grow is something Belle and Betsy do very well!"

This brought laughter from both Grandma Em and Christine as they laid out breakfast. While they ate Emily couldn't help but notice how relaxed Silas was with Christine. Since he was normally quiet around people he didn't know well, she couldn't help but wonder if he was drawn to her because of her resemblance to Julia or if he was attracted to her as a woman. She was lovely and sweet. Grandma Em ate her breakfast with a thoughtful heart.

Later, as Silas helped Christine onto the seat of the sturdy, two-seated wagon, she sighed with relief. If the rest of the family was this nice, everything would be just fine.

The drive to church was short—almost too short for Christine to become nervous; almost, but not quite. Her palms felt damp and she hid them in the folds of her skirt, but the sight of the church interrupted her thoughts.

It was white and small and utterly charming. Christine's eyes traveled skyward, taking in the high steeple. The bell caught the morning sunshine, Christine noticed, just as it began to ring. She loved the sound. Grandma Em's hand on her arm brought her out of her daze and they walked up the steps together. Grandma Em, sensing a need in Christine, closely hooked her arm in Christine's and led them to a seat.

With a simple but warm interior, the oak pews boasted a dark stain, as did the pulpit. Off to one side sat a piano that had seen better days.

Unaware of the curious glances in her direction, Christine's eyes moved around the room. A tall, lovely young woman stood out like a Christmas tree on the Fourth of July in a small town like Baxter!

Christine watched as a man stepped into the pulpit. Emily leaned over and told Christine his name was Pastor Nolan.

Christine listened closely as Pastor Nolan made a few announcements before opening his Bible. She watched Grandma Em do the same with a Bible she hadn't even noticed. Christine's cheeks burned; she had no Bible. Without even looking at Christine, Grandma Em reached into the pew rack, took out a Bible, and handed it calmly to Christine.

It took Christine a little time to find Luke 15:11, and once she did, she didn't look at her Bible again. Her eyes riveted on Pastor Nolan, listening intently to every word.

Pastor Nolan was telling a story of a young man who wanted his inheritance early. His father gave it to him. The young man left home and spent every dime, wasting it away on riotous living. When the young man found himself alone and destitute, and knew his father's servants lived better than he did, he picked himself up and started home. The father had been watching for his son and saw him when he was still down the road. The father ran and hugged his son, his heart alive with joy. They celebrated his homecoming and welcomed him with open arms.

At the end of the sermon Pastor Nolan said, "Maybe one of you has been away from home. The Lord Jesus Christ is watching and waiting to welcome you back. Maybe you aren't sure you even have a home. Maybe you haven't taken that step of faith and told Him of your sin and believed He died for you."

Christine stood for the closing song on wobbly legs, not understanding everything he had said but knowing the part about home was making her depressed and teary. She mentally shook herself lest she cry right there in church.

Moving through church, Grandma Em took Christine with her, introducing her and staying close. Christine was unaware of how conscious Grandma Em was of her feelings. Grandma Em had glanced up at one point to find Mark and Susanne's eyes on Christine. She watched them exchange a glance, and Grandma Em's heart felt heavy for Christine. Emily still knew next to nothing about her, but she knew that when Christine was ready to talk she would be ready to listen.

In the wagon ride home, Christine tried to sort out the people she had met. The sermon, along with all the new faces, had been a bit overwhelming. Plus she still had not met Julia and her family.

Upon arriving, Christine went straight to the kitchen, hoping the work would take her mind off her jumbled emotions.

13

"Well, if that isn't the most depressing sight I know—seeing my dress on another woman and having it look better on her!" Christine spun around in surprise upon hearing these words. Her eyes met those of a beautiful, dark-haired woman.

Julia Cameron MacDonald stood with her hands on her hips trying to look disgusted, but the smile in her eyes told Christine the truth. Julia stepped forward then, hand extended and a full smile lighting her face.

"I'm Julia MacDonald. Gram tells me your name is Christine." Julia shook Christine's hand and both women felt a spark of comradeship. Their relaxation was visible as all doubts cleared.

"Yes, I'm Christine Bennett, and thank you for the dress. I hope it hasn't put you out."

"Julia has enough dresses to loan the entire town and not be put out."

It was a man's voice coming from the kitchen doorway that Julia had just vacated. He was the size of a mountain. Christine stared at him, thinking it was the first time she had met someone bigger than her grandfather. But Julia spoke to him as if she were scolding a child.

"Behave yourself, Mac. Come over here and meet Christine." She caught his hand and pulled him over. "Mac, this is Christine Bennett. Christine, this is my husband, John MacDonald, Mac for short." Christine's hand was swallowed in a huge paw that she could not keep from staring at. Mac, seeing the train of Christine's thoughts, said, "My mother always tells me I just didn't know when to stop growing." He smiled before adding, "I can't say as I meet too many women the height of my Julia." Mac dropped an arm across Julia's shoulders and gave her a quick hug.

Christine smiled at Julia. "I was rather surprised when Susanne brought me a dress that actually fit. You can't know how much I appreciate it."

The next hour was spent in dinner preparation and conversation. Christine met Calvin and Charles, Julia's sons. They had their mother's dark hair and their father's expressive brown eyes.

Content with family surrounding her, Grandma Em bustled around finishing the table with a hug here and a word there. Christine was again amazed at how accepted she was. When Susanne and Mark arrived, Emily bounced into the kitchen to hug Christine and inform her of her upcoming fourth birthday. Then she raced off to find Calvin and Charles.

Dinner was wonderful—with only one embarrassing moment. Mark prayed, thanking God for the day, the food, and the addition of Christine to the family. Immediately upon the heels of the "Amen," Emily wanted to know if Christine was now a member of the family because she was wearing Aunt Julia's dress.

Seeing Christine's flaming cheeks and Mark about to reprimand Emily, Grandma Em broke in kindly and explained that Christine was family because they loved her and wanted her to be.

Readying herself for bed, Christine reflected on the long day. She had read a story to the children and also listened to Julia and Susanne talk about babies and pregnancies. Mark had stopped her at one point to ask after her shoulder. She assured him everything was fine.

Silas had been quiet until Grandma Em announced that she and Christine were going to paint the porch this week. Everyone save Julia protested. Conversation was frenzied for nearly 20 minutes, when Silas ended with "Luke wouldn't like this, Gram, and I think you know it. I also think you know, if he were here, he'd put a stop to this idea in a hurry." But the determined look on Grandma Em's face told them they had all wasted their breath.

Reasoning that Luke must be the oldest and the head of the family, Christine wasn't too sure she would like anyone who was at all hard on Grandma Em. But then she realized she was being silly and unfair; Luke probably loved his grandmother very much. She would reserve judgment until she met the man.

Christine now lay in the darkness waiting for sleep to come. Pastor Nolan's words came back to her. "Maybe you aren't sure you even have a home." Home! The thought brought a fresh pain to Christine's chest. She would finish that letter to Mrs. Hall and get it off soon. The thought helped ease the ache in the region of her heart as she drifted off to sleep.

14

The next two weeks were joyful and busy. The painting of the porch and shutters went off without a hitch. Grandma Em was thrilled, though her grandsons were still doubtful.

Emily's birthday party was held at Grandma Em's one Saturday afternoon. Emily's special guest that day was Mr. Turley, Grandma Em's neighbor. Emily usually saw Mr. Turley when she was at her great-grandmother's. The man's kindness and lack of a grandfather in her own life made him a special asset.

Julia came one afternoon. Leaving Calvin and Charles with Grandma Em, she whisked Christine back to the farm to go riding. Christine was more than a little surprised when Julia took her upstairs for riding clothes and handed her a pair of men's jeans. Christine looked down at the jeans and then back to Julia's mirth-filled eyes. Both women broke out in uproarious laughter.

The MacDonald land adjoined the Cameron land, and as the women rode over the wide acres with joyous abandon, it occurred to Christine to ask Julia how Mac felt about her in men's pants, thinking back to her grandfather's reaction. But she thought better of it and kept quiet.

Christine mailed her letter to Mrs. Hall, explaining briefly her situation and that she was well. Christine asked many questions in the letter, making it hard to sit and wait for a reply.

One day brought a confrontation between Christine and Mark, when she insisted upon knowing the balance of her medical bill. Mark assured her there was no hurry, but Christine was adamant. Taking nearly every dime of her first wages from Grandma Em, Christine made her first payment. Mark protested right up to the time she left his office, but to no avail. As he saw her out the door and

62

watched her walk up the street, he realized why Grandma Em and Julia liked her so much: They were three of a kind.

After nearly three weeks in Baxter, Christine was settled and content. Much of the time she was too busy to think of Spooner and its troubles.

Three weeks with the Cameron family was bringing changes to Christine's life. She was very aware that they were something special. At first she attributed it to a big family and many friends, something she had never had. But as time went on it was obvious there was something more. Not having heard from Mrs. Hall, Christine could only hope she would be around long enough to find out what that something was. But for now she was at peace and was more than content to stay where she was.

15

Luke Cameron shifted his weight on the train seat. Why did the last 50 miles to Baxter always feel like the longest? Deliberately taking a night train out of Chicago, it had given him one more day with Paul, and he figured he could sleep on board.

But he had figured wrong. Luke had only dozed, and now he felt achy and irritable. The train was due to arrive in Baxter before breakfast. He realized as he sat there, that it would be hours before he could crawl between the sheets of his own bed. His own bed! The thought brought a smile to his lips. At his height he really missed the length of the specially made bed. It had belonged to his parents, Joseph and Kathrine Cameron, who had both been very tall.

As usual, whenever Luke thought of his parents and the wonderful marriage they had, it brought a painful ache to his chest over his own single state.

He and Mark were both 28 years old. God had seen fit to give Mark a wife. He had also been blessed with Emily, and now another baby was due very soon. Luke felt a bit envious, but had decided long ago that God's will was best. With this acceptance came the desire to live to the fullest, alone or not. This submission, nevertheless, did not deter Luke from praying for the desire of his heart.

At one time he prayed simply for a wife. But the years passed and no feelings of love developed for any of the young women at church. This caused Luke's prayer to change, and he began to pray for preparation. Daily he prayed for growth and wisdom, asking God to help him be ready if ever God chose to give him a wife.

Another thing Luke did over the years was to observe. The two marriages he was closest to were those of his brother and sister. After much time watching Mark with

Susanne and Mac with Julia, Luke was sure that God would give him a wife like Susanne. Sue was sweet, gentle, and submissive. Luke loved his sister Julia, but she certainly had a mind of her own. He wondered at times if Mac had any control over her at all.

Luke remembered back to a time when Julia was 12 years old. She had put on a pair of boy's jeans, sneaked out of the house, and gone riding astride. She had gotten in trouble for it, but it had never stopped her. In fact, she was still doing it. Why, just a few days before Luke had left for Chicago, Julia had ridden over, in blue jeans, astride her horse. Luke had stared at her jean-clad legs in tight-lipped disapproval, causing the happy smile on Julia's face to vanish.

That she had come over especially to have a quiet visit with him before he left for his trip only occurred to him after, without dismounting, Julia handed him a basket of his favorite cookies and then with a quiet "I'll miss you, Luke," pulled her horse around and rode away.

Luke, awash with guilt, knew he had to see her and make things right. So after supper he rode over to the MacDonald farm, only to be told by Mac that Julia had gone to bed early with a headache.

Mac stood watching his brother-in-law run long fingers through dark curly hair in mild frustration. Mac was reasonably sure that Luke was the reason Julia had come home from her ride with red, swollen eyes. As strong-willed as Julia was, Luke's approval had always been important to her. Luke was also a bit too stern for his own good.

Luke had not been able to see Julia to apologize until the night of her birthday party. Smiling, she told him it didn't matter, but Luke could see the hurt she was trying so hard to hide.

Luke's hand went to the bag on the seat next to him. He hoped Julia would like the book and small glass dish he had found for her in Chicago. He planned on telling her again how sorry he was, and hopefully they could then have the talk they were cheated out of because of his thoughtless-ness.

The dish he had bought for Julia brought his thoughts back to Chicago and Caroline. Caroline Chambers. Luke had been staying with Frank and Lily Chambers. Their massive ranch housed more than 200 head of horses. The same day Luke decided which horses he wanted, Caroline, the Chambers' 17-year-old daughter, returned from a visit to her cousins.

Luke had liked her instantly. She was small and blonde, with a bubbly, talkative personality. The two had gone riding and for walks. When Luke was ready to go and stay with Paul, Caroline had talked him into returning for her eighteenth birthday party that weekend.

Luke had had a wonderful time at the party, feeling more drawn to Caroline as the evening progressed. But the next morning, when Luke attended church with the Chambers family, he felt terribly let down. The church was large, but only about half the pews were filled. Luke listened as the minister read a single Bible verse, shut the Book, and never once referred back to it. His monotone voice droned on and on about the sinful state of the city, but not once did he mention the fact that Jesus Christ died for those sinners.

Frank Chambers slept through the entire service. Each time Luke glanced at Caroline she was looking at him, making him wonder how much of the sermon she had heard.

Later Caroline begged Luke to write. Luke had not com-mitted himself and had only smiled at her, even when she grabbed his hand, pressing her address into his palm. Luke wondered a bit at the mixture of relief and regret he felt as he left.

Luke's visit with Paul had been wonderful. Paul's natural speaking ability was popular on campus, and even though he was still in school, he had already been asked to fill the pulpit at several small churches. His enthusiasm was catch-ing, making it even harder for Luke to leave. The men had embraced for long moments, knowing that it would probably be Christmas before Paul got home again.

It was getting light out now, and Luke could see the countryside. He guessed the train to be within 20 miles of Baxter. "It's beautiful up in our neck of the woods," Luke had told Frank Chambers one evening. Frank decided then and there that he and the Mrs. needed a little time away and that they would deliver the horses together. They would be up in a few weeks; Luke was to wait for a wire.

As the train pulled into Baxter, Luke stood and stretched his cramped muscles. He couldn't keep the smile from his face as his long legs carried him toward Grandma Em's. It felt so good to be home!

16

"Okay, Caesar, you're all set." Christine patted the rump of the big horse and moved toward the high-pitched bleat of Chester, wondering as she did why she never fed the goat first just to keep him quiet. As usual, the din came to an instant halt the moment Chester got his food.

The chickens were happily pecking at their meal as Christine headed around the barn to Belle and Betsy's pen. Both were overjoyed to see her, crowding near Christine's legs as though they were starved. Christine filled the trough and turned to go. Betsy, in her eagerness, rushed to the trough and bumped Christine on the back of the legs. She reacted quickly, dropping the pail and reaching for the fence. Catching it kept her from going facedown into the pig muck, but her knees buckled and she felt them sink deeply.

Having struggled out of the pen, Christine stood and surveyed the damage. The front of her dress was ruined. She watched as the slime dripped onto her boots, and she had to put her hand down to hold the dress away from her legs. She knew she had never smelled worse. Christine shot an angry look at Betsy, but the sow was head and ears into the slop, oblivious to all else.

Muttering under her breath about the tasty dishes made from ham, Christine retrieved her pail and stormed toward the house. Rounding the barn, she ran headlong into a tall, solid body. Christine gasped in surprise and stepped back. Her eyes shot downward and saw boots and pants liberally smeared with muck before looking up to the surprised face staring down at her.

"Oh, Mark, it's you! I'm sorry," Christine wailed. "Look at what I've done to your pants and boots. What a mess!" Christine plucked at the ruined skirt. "It was Betsy. She bumped right into me. I tell you, sometimes those pigs make me furious." Christine's anger made her speak quickly and gesture wildly with her arms, the pail in one hand swinging as she spoke. "Well," she said with an angry shrug, "the damage is done. Come up to the house and I'll try to clean up your boots."

Christine then stalked off with a determined stride, pail still swinging, leaving the confused man to follow in her odorous wake.

Grandma Em stepped out of the house just as they approached the back steps. "Oh, no, Christine, your dress! Which one was it?" Her voice sounded resigned.

"Betsy," Christine answered with disgust.

"Oh, Christine, I'm sorry. Betsy is always so pushy." Grandma Em looked at the man standing behind Christine. His confused face and mud-spattered clothing greatly amused her. Her voice told him as much when she said, "Welcome home, Luke."

Christine, who had been wiping ineffectively at her skirt, looked sharply at Grandma Em's face. Her eyes moved slowly to the man she had just plowed into and covered with pig muck. Her face began to burn as the full realization hit: This was not Mark Cameron. This was not the man who had nursed her back to health, befriended her, found her a job, and then took her lovingly into his own family.

This was *Luke*, the brother who had been on a buying trip in Chicago. Only he was no longer in Chicago—he was here, and Christine had welcomed him home by ruining his pants. Christine stared hard at his face. Why had no one mentioned that Mark and Luke were identical twins? It was unbelievable that two faces could be so much alike. She continued to stare rudely until Grandma Em finally broke into her thoughts.

"Christine?" Still she stared on, and Luke began to feel irritated with her.

"Christine?" Christine turned with a guilty start. "This is Luke, my oldest grandson. Luke, this is Christine Bennett. She lives here and works for me."

Luke's eyes widened at this bit of information, but he recovered quickly and offered his hand. "It's a pleasure to meet you, Christine." His voice was extremely polite.

Christine's own hand came forward to return the shake, but upon seeing how muddy it was, she quickly put it behind her back. Luke's hand was extended expectantly in midair until he finally dropped it to his side. "It's nice to meet you also." Christine's voice was stiff and her face was ablaze once again. Years of training came to the fore as Luke and Christine made an attempt to remember their manners in such an awkward situation. But Christine could take no more and turned quickly to Grandma Em. "I'll go clean up." Without waiting for a reply, she nearly ran up the steps and into the kitchen.

Luke, who was left standing outside with Grandma Em, reached into his pocket for his handkerchief. "Would you care to explain what this is all about, Gram?" Luke's voice was quiet as he used his handkerchief to wipe his face, his nose wrinkling as the smell from his boots traveled upward.

Grandma Em took pity. "Let's get you cleaned up and we'll talk over breakfast."

Nearly an hour later she concluded, "So you see, Luke, it doesn't matter that I don't know all about Christine, including why she is so far from home. Although she has not shared with me, she has talked with Mark. But if I learned one thing being a doctor's wife for over 45 years, you don't ask questions about patients." Grandma Em paused and put her hand over Luke's. "What I do know is that right now I need her, and I hope her need for me will lead her to Christ."

Luke was quiet for some time. "I guess the idea takes a little getting used to. All these years of fighting to remain alone and independent, and in the three weeks I'm gone you capitulate and let someone not only work for you but live here as well."

"If it makes you feel any better, Mark sounded just like

you the day he came and told me his idea for Christine working and living here."

This brought a smile to Luke's face. Luke had, without spoken word, become head of the family when, over four years ago, Joseph Cameron had died. Emily was always a very capable woman, and Luke did not move in and take over. He was simply there when she needed him. Mark and Mac were more than willing to lend a hand, but Luke and Silas, being bachelors, were more available.

Emily rarely had words with her grandson, but when she did, Luke usually won. In an infuriatingly logical way he stated his case. He preferred to deal in facts rather than emotions, and much to Emily's chagrin, he could talk circles around her.

Luke was usually very sensitive to his grandmother's needs and wishes. Along the way there had been a few times when he had simply put his foot right down on the top of some of her plans.

Luke now sat on the wagon seat beside Silas. He felt strangely humbled at the thought of how well things went with him not around. He realized that he and Grandma Em hadn't really finished their conversation when Silas had shown up and offered Luke a ride home.

Silas hadn't known the time Luke's train was to arrive— just the day. But Silas was like that. In his quiet way he seemed to sense when and where he was needed and then just stepped in without pomp or ceremony.

As the wagon neared the ranch, the restless night was quickly catching up to Luke. Suddenly he couldn't quite remember what he had been a bit uneasy about at Grandma Em's. Oh, well, he would think on it later. Right now the ranch was in view, and he was sure Silas wouldn't mind if he got in a quick nap. Whatever today's problems were, they would wait a few more hours.

— ✦ —

"You say you received this letter today?"

"Yes, Sheriff," replied Mrs. Hall, relief and concern evident in her voice.

The sheriff turned back to the piece of paper in his hand.

Dear Mrs. Hall:

I'm sorry for the worry and pain you must certainly have experienced these past weeks. I am also sorry I was not able to tell you of my plans before leaving. The letter you delivered from Carl Maxwell told me to leave Spooner immediately. I was to meet someone in Fall Creek. When this didn't work out, I stayed on the train and ended up in a small town called Baxter. I live with and work for an older woman. She and her family are very kind and loving to me. I am physically settled but my heart and mind await answers. Please ask Carl to write me. I need his help. I'll close by telling you once again that I am fine. I hope this finds you well. I miss you. Take care and please write to me so I know you received this letter.

Much love,

Christie

P.S. My address: Christine Bennett
c/o Mrs. Emily Cameron
Baxter, Wisconsin

"Mrs. Hall, has anyone else seen this letter?"

"No, I brought it right to you."

The sheriff nodded and stood still as though in deep thought. When he spoke, his voice was very quiet. "You heard that Carl Maxwell is missing?"

"I'd heard."

"Without him to question, the only place to go is back to Christine." He paused. "Write her and tell her to stay where she is. Tell her Carl is missing and that until I can dig a bit deeper, she's better off where she is. And of course, warn her about talking to people. The less said, the better. You of course understand it is just as necessary here."

"Of course, Sheriff." Mrs. Hall put out her hand to take the letter, but the sheriff held it away.

"I'd really like to keep this." He saw Mrs. Hall's hesitation and then continued. "I'll copy the address so you can write, but this letter is important."

She nodded reluctantly and replied, "When you're done with it, I'd like it back."

"Of course, Mrs. Hall; I'll keep it safe. Now look on the bright side. Christine has written, and you know she's safe. We'll get to the bottom of this. Don't you worry."

Mrs. Hall thanked the sheriff and he watched her walk away, wishing he felt as optimistic as he sounded.

17

Christine stood in the parlor before the large family portrait that Grandma Em had just asked her to hang. Twins! Why had no one ever mentioned that Mark and Luke were identical twins? Shaking her head, she wondered how many times she had asked herself that question.

Yesterday had been awful. Christine could not stop thinking about how foolish she felt while meeting Luke.

Christine's eyes moved intently over the portrait. The four Cameron brothers stood in the back. Susanne, Mac, and Julia were seated in front, a child in each lap. Silas stood to the far right of the back row, sporting a beard as full then as it was today. The man next to him could be none other than Paul. Dark hair, boyish good looks, and most of all his height marked him as a Cameron. By simple deduction Christine guessed the next man to be Luke. To the far left stood Mark, his hand on Sue's shoulder, a small Emily in her lap. Judging from the changes in Emily, Calvin, and Charles, the picture was probably about two years old.

Her eyes once again centered on the identical men in the back row, glancing quickly back and forth between the two. They were even of the same height and build. Well, possibly not. Maybe Luke's shoulders were a bit wider. Christine turned away from the picture with an angry shrug. What did she care if his shoulders were bigger? If she never saw the man again it would be way too soon. Deciding to put it behind her, Christine walked into the dining room to dust, unaware of Grandma Em standing in the doorway to the kitchen, watching the emotions play across Christine's face.

Grandma Em could feel Christine's frustration. Yesterday must have been terribly embarrassing for her. The look on Christine's face when Grandma Em welcomed Luke home clearly stated that she had taken him for Mark. And who wouldn't? There were only a handful of people who could tell them apart.

Grandma Em's mind went to the conversation yesterday. They hadn't really finished talking, leaving Grandma Em unsure just how Luke felt about Christine.

As Grandma Em continued to ponder, it occurred to her why this was so unsettling. Luke's opinion was of the utmost importance to her. If Luke felt uncomfortable with Christine or disapproved of her in some way, she wanted to know. Grandma Em quickly reined in her wild thoughts. God did not put Christine in their lives simply to pluck her back out again. God would handle it. His timing would be perfect. Emily went back to work quoting Proverbs 3:5,6: "Trust in the Lord with all thine heart, and lean not unto thine own understanding. In all thy ways acknowledge him, and he shall direct thy paths."

18

"You haven't stopped smiling since you got back." Silas' voice broke through Luke's concentration.

Luke did not bother to deny it. His grin just widened and his eyes once again swept over the acres he called home— the same acres in fact that his father, Joseph Cameron Jr., called home, as well as his mother's father, Charles Langley, before him.

Supper over and the dishes done, Luke and Silas were settled on the back porch. The silence they shared was comfortable, each letting the peace and serenity of the evening settle around him.

Sunday mornings brought extra work, with Grandma Em's chores to be done as well as all their own stock to feed, so Saturday evening was usually spent relaxing and then retiring to bed early.

Luke broke the silence with a question that told Silas what had been on his mind. "Si, has Christine been going to church with you and Gram?"

"Yes."

Luke merely nodded and left Silas to ponder on what had brought this up. He would have been surprised if he had been able to read Luke's mind, since his question had been nothing more than a passing thought, not centered on Christine, but on going to church and the day he had attended services with Caroline.

Luke remembered a time in his life when, in his teen years, church had not been one of his favorite places. Caroline, he had to admit, seemed more interested in him than in the sermon. He couldn't help but feel a bit flattered until he remembered how easily the minister had made it to think of anything besides the sermon. He was still praying about writing her, his heart still very unsure of his feelings for her. He also prayed he would not feel desperate—that his wanting a wife so badly wouldn't cloud his mind and make him forget that God's will was more important than his own. Once again, as Luke surrendered his will to God's a peace settled over his troubled heart. He knew without a doubt that if God had a wife for him and he left the choosing in His hands, everything would be perfect.

In town Grandma Em and Christine were also finished with supper. Settled in the parlor, Christine picked up some mending and Grandma Em chose a book. Grandma Em had held her tongue all evening even though she could tell something was bothering Christine. After pretending to read for a full five minutes, she gave up and plunged in.

"Christine, you seem a bit quiet this evening. I hope you're not coming down with something."

"No, Grandma Em, I'm fine." They both knew this wasn't true.

Grandma Em plunged in again, praying she wasn't being too pushy. "Was the letter you received today from home?"

"Yes." Grandma Em watched an expression she couldn't quite define pass over Christine's face.

"Would you like to talk about it?" Grandma Em was surprised when Christine didn't even hesitate.

"It's rather complicated, Grandma Em. You see, I didn't leave Spooner under the best of circumstances. Being here, working and getting drawn into your family a little more each week, sometimes causes me to forget that there are things at home that need to be settled." Christine paused here, and the emotion on her face became clear to Emily. Fear! Christine searched Grandma Em's face intently before continuing hesitantly. "The woman who wrote me, a woman I trust, advised me to stay here for the time being ... and, well, we've never discussed how long you need me. If this is a temporary arrangement or..." her voice trailed off.

Grandma Em's eyes flooded with tears. When she could speak, her voice was very soft. "Were it in my power, Christine, I would keep you here with me for the rest of my life."

Christine flew into the arms of the older woman.

Christine clung to Emily as great sobs racked her young body and Emily's own tears ran silently down her cheeks. Christine's tears seemed to exhaust her, and so, with a final hug for Grandma Em and a hoarse "thank you," she took the stairs to bed.

Once in bed, exhausted as she was, Christine could not keep her mind off the letter from Mrs. Hall. Even as sleep claimed her, snatches of the letter returned. "Carl Maxwell is missing. Talk to no one. The sheriff is looking into things. Stay where you are. I repeat, talk to no one."

— ✛ —

"You mean to tell me you've been gone all this time, only to return and tell me the job isn't done? How long does it take to kill one woman?" Vince Jeffers' face was mottled with rage. The veins in his neck stood out like cords.

"I'm sorry, Mr. Jeffer's sir, but no one has seen a girl of that description, and the only Mr. Franklin in town somebody said was killed by a runaway horse a few weeks back."

Vince Jeffers was so angry he wanted to strike the man. He stood behind his desk, a heavy glass paperweight clenched in his hand.

Finally he spoke through gritted teeth. "Get out! I need time to think, and don't you dare show your face around me until I send for you!"

The man needed no further prodding. He bolted for the door, nearly frightened out of his wits by his employer's rage. The sound of shattering glass echoed in his ears as he made good his escape.

19

Emily sat on the side of her bed feeling every day of her 70 years. Last night had been awful. She had gone to bed feeling very good about being able to reassure Christine of her job and a place to live, only to be wakened sometime near midnight by her screams.

By the time Emily got to Christine's room, she had stopped screaming. Emily found her sitting up in bed, her eyes glazed over and soaked with perspiration. Grandma Em lit the lamp and took Christine's hand, holding it gently until she noticed her presence.

"He was trying to kill you." Christine's voice was a dry whisper.

"Who was, dear?"

"Vince Jeffers. He had stabbed Mrs. Hall and was going after you. I couldn't stop him." Her voice broke.

"A dream, Christine; it was just a dream. I'm safe and you're safe. It's all right now." Grandma Em rose and brought a damp cloth to bathe Christine's face. She helped her into a fresh nightgown, all the time talking in a calm, reassuring voice. When Christine settled back in bed, Grandma Em blew out the light and once again took her hand. In a quiet, clear, trusting voice she began to pray. "Dear heavenly Father, please cover her with Your loving comfort. Help her to relax and sleep. Help her to forget her fear and trust You to watch over her this night. Thank You, God, for giving Christine to us. Help me to be here for her and to comfort her in any way I can. Thank You, God. Amen."

Christine's eyes had closed. Emily's hand reached to smooth her brow. Her heart filled with anguish over this young woman's pain. Emily sat with her for awhile before making her way back to her own bed. Sleep did not come until nearly dawn.

With all these thoughts going through Grandma Em's mind, she was shocked to find Christine up ahead of her with coffee on and breakfast started.

"Christine, I'm surprised you're up. When I didn't hear you moving around in your room, I assumed you were getting some extra rest."

"I was awake and I just got up." Christine's smile was meant to reassure Grandma Em, but she wasn't fooled.

They worked for a few minutes in silence until Christine spoke. "I feel rather foolish for waking you last night. I've never done anything like that before. I'm sorry."

"Christine, there is no reason to apologize. It's not as if you planned to have a bad dream that scared you senseless." Grandma Em chided her a bit sternly. And then more gently, "Do you want to talk about it?"

The back door opened at that moment, keeping Christine from answering. Grandma Em sent her a look of apology for the interruption and then went to greet her grandsons.

Forgetting that Luke was also a regular guest on Sunday morning, she turned to add more eggs to the pan. Christine no longer felt embarrassed about their first meeting. She realized over the past week that these things just happen.

No, her thoughts this morning were not on Luke, but Mark. She had lain awake most of the night and after much thought had decided to talk with Mark. So far the sheriff had not talked to her, and frankly, she preferred it that way. She much preferred confiding in Mark and letting him decide if and when to talk with the sheriff.

Christine, her thoughts so intense, hadn't realized that Grandma Em had taken Silas into the parlor to show him some new sheet music. Luke sat down silently at the table to await the coffee.

Christine bustled around and finally moved to the table to pour coffee. Not until she was nearly on top of Luke did she realize he was there. Having those startling blue eyes leveled so intently on her face caused Christine's hand to shake, splashing some coffee on Luke's leg. Luke was on his feet in an instant and reaching for a napkin.

Christine stood, the pot now upright, a trembling hand pressed to her mouth in horror. "I'm sorry—are you burned, are you hurt? How clumsy of me! I didn't see you, I'm sorry." The words tumbled out and Christine turned to replace the pot and get a damp cloth.

Luke wondered, as she did, if it was at all safe to be around this woman. He couldn't quite squelch the irritation he felt at having his Sunday pants stained. It was either wear them as they were or go all the way home and change.

Christine returned and handed Luke a wet cloth, seeing as she did that his napkin had been of little help. Not until Luke returned the cloth to her did he see the tears standing in her wide, green eyes. He couldn't have known that lost sleep and worry had brought them on and not just the spilled coffee. Upon seeing them, Luke's irritation drained away.

"I'm sorry, are you burned?"

"No, just a bit damp." He smiled and indicated his pants, hoping she would believe him.

When she just stood there, blushing and looking miserable, he tried again. "Honestly, Christine, I'm not burned; I'm fine, really."

She stared at him a moment more and then with a little nod turned back to the stove, wiping her eyes with the backs of her hands.

Luke thought that for as tall as she was, such a childlike gesture made her look like a lost little girl. He felt sorry for her and hoped she hadn't seen any of his earlier irritation.

When Grandma Em and Silas returned, they all sat down to breakfast. All three of the Camerons noticed Christine pushing her food around her plate. Grandma Em and Luke felt sure they knew why. Silas just felt concern for her.

20

Within the next hour the four of them were sitting in church together. As Silas parked the horses and wagon, Christine had a chance to see Susanne and tell her she needed to speak with Mark. Susanne hugged Christine and promised to pass the word along. Having Mark and Susanne to talk with was a great help.

But these thoughts were far from Christine's mind as she sat in church beside Grandma Em. As usual, she listened intently to Pastor Nolan speak, wondering as before at the strange feeling of expectancy she always felt.

Christine reached for the pew Bible when Pastor Nolan told them today's text was in Luke 19. Her eyebrows rose in surprise, for she hadn't remembered that Luke was a Bible name.

In Luke 19 Pastor Nolan told about Zacchaeus, a tax collector who cheated people. This made him very rich but not very well liked. He was also short. On this particular day in Scripture, Jesus was coming to the town where Zacchaeus lived. Zacchaeus wanted to see Him, but the crowd and Zacchaeus' short height made this impossible.

So the little man ran further down the road where Jesus would be walking. The Bible said that Zacchaeus climbed into a tree and waited for Jesus to pass.

When Jesus was below the tree, He looked up and saw Zacchaeus. "Come down quickly," Jesus bade the man; "today I'm going to eat at your house."

Christine's mind wandered a bit as she wondered how Jesus knew that Zacchaeus was in the tree. She continued to wonder about this even as the pastor spoke on Zacchaeus giving back four times the amount of money he had overcharged people, and giving half his goods to the poor. The final verse was Luke 19:10: "For the Son of man has come to seek and to save that which was lost."

As everyone reached for their hymnbooks and stood for the closing song, Christine kept the pew Bible in her hand. She read the passage once again as everyone sang, thinking as she read that she had missed the part where Zacchaeus called down to Jesus or made himself known in some other way.

The service ended and everyone moved toward the door—everyone except Christine and Luke. Christine was still reading, and Luke, who had sat on the inside of the pew against the wall, couldn't exit without climbing over her. He stood patiently, waiting for her to finish.

When Christine read the passage through for the second time, she turned abruptly to Luke. "How did Jesus know Zacchaeus was in the tree?"

Luke, who was half expecting something like this, answered quietly, "Because God knows everything."

He could see this made no sense whatever to Christine because her brow was knit with confusion. He continued, "And Jesus is God's Son. Jesus is God." Luke watched her face, unsure of what was so confusing.

Christine opened her Bible again and said, "But where does it say that?"

Luke finally understood. "It doesn't say that in the passage we were in today. Here, let me show you where it does say that." Luke opened his own Bible and began to thumb through it.

As he did so, Christine realized that the church had emptied. How embarrassing! She had stood there reading even though the service was over, and Luke couldn't even get out of the pew until she moved!

"No, Luke, it's all right. I best get to the wagon."

Luke looked up to see Christine's face flushed in a way that was becoming familiar to him. Her movements as she headed toward the aisle were stiff, and she was looking anywhere but at him.

"Christine." His deep voice stopped her just as she reached the aisle. Luke waited until she faced him before speaking. "After lunch today, if you'd like, I'll write some verses down and you can look them up yourself."

She nearly sagged with relief. With a nod and a small smile she headed for the door.

Luke replaced the pew Bible that Christine had dropped in her hurry to escape. He followed, his pace more sedate as he exited, belying the way his mind raced for verses she would understand and, more importantly, would whet her appetite for more.

21

The scene on the front porch was a peaceful one. Story time was over and Emily's small head rested on her mother's round stomach. Susanne's foot kept the porch swing at a steady rock.

Emily's eyes slid shut for the last time and Susanne's hand moved to stroke her shiny curls. She smiled as she realized it wouldn't bother her in the least to have another little blonde girl. Her other hand moved absently over her stomach.

The front door opened and shut quietly. Luke took a seat near the swing and sat in silence, watching his niece sleep. A frown crossed his face as he saw Sue's hand on her abdomen. Luke opened his mouth to speak, but Sue was observant and ready for him.

"I'm fine."

Luke relaxed and smiled. "Can Mark hide anything from you?"

"Nope, not a thing."

"How long now?"

"Mark says two weeks. I say sooner."

"He's the doctor."

"So he keeps reminding me." Sue answered with a smile and a raise of her eyebrows.

Luke laughed softly before asking. "Where is Mark?"

Sue nodded her head toward a huge old willow tree that stood some distance off the corner of the porch. Amid bare switches hanging nearly to the ground, Mark and Christine could be seen and were obviously in deep conversation.

— ✣ —

"Your grandmother assured me last night when we talked that I have a job and a place to live for an indefinite period of time. It's good to have that worry off my mind. I plan to write Mrs. Hall so her mind is at ease."

Mark nodded. "Our sheriff spoke to me about contacting the law in Spooner, just so the lines of communication are open. Both towns need to work together on this."

Christine shook her head sadly. "I just don't understand. Grandpa was not a wealthy man. I mean, we lived comfortably and I had all I needed, but it just doesn't make sense."

"I must admit, it's all rather strange. What we know isn't much. First a note to you from Carl Maxwell, and then the man disappears."

"And don't forget my grandfather's will leaving everything to Vince Jeffers in the event of my death. I'm only 19 years old! He would never have written that. Another thing puzzles me—my grandfather's charity. It was never even mentioned. He gave often and quite generously to a small orphanage in Spooner. It doesn't make sense that he wouldn't even remember them."

The two stood together for a moment in thoughtful silence. Mark studied once again the letter in his hand. "Christine," he began gently, "when a person passes away, it's normal for the surviving family members to go through the loved one's possessions. If you were home, I'm sure you would have already started this, painful though it may be." Mark hesitated, wanting to be tactful. "When you write to Mrs. Hall, why not ask her to look through your grandfather's things? I realize this is highly personal, but maybe she can turn up something that will give us some answers."

As Mark suspected, Christine did not jump at the idea. It still upset her to think about the finality of her grandfather's death. So Mark hastened to add, "What you write is up to you. You don't have to tell me your decision—it was only a suggestion. If it's all right, though, I'd like to show this letter to the sheriff when I see him."

"That's fine, Mark." Christine's voice was preoccupied. "Will you please tell Grandma Em I've gone for a walk and I'll be gone awhile?"

"Sure, I'll tell her."

The words were barely out of his mouth before Christine walked away. The need inside her to escape was so desperate that she nearly ran. Cutting across Mr. Turley's field, her long legs carried her swiftly to a quiet spot along the creek which she had discovered during her first week at Grandma Em's.

An enormous boulder at the edge of the water was Christine's destination. Sinking down to it with a weary plop, Christine let the afternoon sun beat upon her. She welcomed its warmth, though it crossed her mind that she should have worn a hat. She studied the backs of her hands: brown. It was what she got for working in the garden without gloves.

A sudden movement interrupted her reverie. Christine's eyes were drawn to the creek's edge. A fish had swum between the rocks and was trapped in a pool barely large enough to hold him.

Christine contemplated the situation a moment before reaching out to shift one of the large rocks. The hoped-for result was immediate: With a flip of its tail the fish headed downstream. With envy Christine's eyes followed as it moved swiftly out of sight in its newfound freedom.

Freedom. It seemed like forever since Christine had experienced that feeling. Freedom to go home if she wanted. Freedom from worries and fears. A freedom that, up until the time of her grandfather's death, she had taken for granted.

Christine felt a lonely ache within her. Luke said that God knows everything. Did He know why she sometimes felt empty inside? Did He care? So many questions but no answers. Christine ached for her grandfather's presence, yet she knew her pride was keeping her from asking for help. So the afternoon shadows lengthened and Christine sat with only her tears for company.

— ✦ —

Back at the house, Luke and Silas had their suit coats on and were headed for the door. After kissing Grandma Em, Luke handed her a piece of paper. He explained about the verses, and Grandma Em assured him that Christine would get them.

— ✣ —

For Mrs. Hall, Sunday afternoon was usually spent visiting her sister and family. Mrs. Hall's spirits had been up ever since she had heard from Christine. So, after a good meal and a visit with her sister, Mrs. Hall started walking out to the Bennett residence with a light step.

"Good afternoon, Mrs. Hall."

"Oh! Mr. Jeffers, good afternoon to you! It's lovely, is it not?" Mrs. Hall smiled at him.

"Yes, indeed it is. May I wish you also a splendid week."

"Why, thank you, Mr. Jeffers." Mrs. Hall continued on her way.

Vince sat astride his bay stallion and watched the woman's light step, wondering at her exuberance. She certainly didn't look like the grieving woman he had seen before. Maybe she had had news of Christine.

Vince heeled his horse into a walk. He had finally cooled off from his last meeting with that incompetent fool who worked for him. Maybe it was time to send for him again.

Once again in the Bennett house, Mrs. Hall hung up her bonnet and changed her shoes. It was then that she put her finger on what was different about Vince Jeffers.

She had grown used to his smile, a smile that never quite reached his eyes. He was so different from Mr. Bennett that it was a wonder they had ever formed a partnership. But that wasn't it. What was it, then, that was troubling her about him? *He had stopped her and talked to her but didn't even ask after Christine.* How odd! Rarely had he ever given her the time of day.

Once again Mrs. Hall experienced that strange feeling that she got whenever she saw Vince Jeffers lately, as if there were something she was supposed to tell him or remember that she couldn't quite come up with.

Mrs. Hall did a mental shrug as she reached for *A Study in Scarlet*, the new Sherlock Holmes mystery novel that her sister had just finished. Whatever it was with Vince Jeffers would have to wait until tomorrow.

22

"This week has just flown by, especially since the weather has finally cooled." Grandma Em shifted. "Did you get your letter off?"

"Yes, it's been posted. I also had another confrontation with your grandson. Why does he put up such a fuss when I try to pay on my bill?"

Grandma Em laughed but offered no explanation. The truth of the matter was that Mark's heart was tender to a fault. He and Sue cared deeply for Christine and would do anything to ease her plight. Grandma Em also knew about pride. She knew Christine had plenty of it because she saw herself so clearly in the young woman.

The women were now on Grandma Em's street, her house in sight.

"Is that Luke on your porch?"

"Yes, I believe so." Something in Grandma Em's voice made Christine ask, "Do you think something is wrong?"

Grandma Em slowed down a bit and spoke softly. "Don't ask me how I know, Christine, but I think I'm about to get in trouble for painting my own porch."

Near the porch now, the women exchanged a glance and then quickly looked away lest they should begin to laugh. The days they had spent painting had been wonderful. Getting to know and trust each other through paint spatters and laughter had been a tonic to Christine. Neither woman would have traded the experience for the world.

"Hello, Luke. You're in time for lunch. Will you stay?"

Luke answered as he took his grandmother's packages and held the door for both ladies. "Thanks, Gram."

As lunch preparations were made, Christine was aware of Luke's eyes. They settled on both her and Grandma Em for long, intense moments. The conversation was light, but Luke seemed somewhat distracted.

The three made short work of thick ham slices, fresh-made bread, and cheese wedges. The peaches were ripe to perfection, sweet as candy.

A forkful of chocolate cake was halfway to Grandma Em's mouth when Luke said offhandedly, "I heard today that Lars Larson broke his arm." Luke watched as the women across from him paused ever so slightly in their eating before rushing on, taking care not to look anywhere but at their plates.

Luke felt a sinking sensation in the pit of his stomach. Their pause had confirmed the gossip he had heard downtown to be true.

"Did you know he had broken his arm, Gram?"

"Yes."

"Was he able to get to your porch and shutters before he fell?"

"No, he was not." Her answer was quiet, but firm.

Luke's own eyes dropped to his plate. He was beginning to wish he hadn't even asked. A fight with his grandmother was not what he wanted, but one look at her face told him he had best step carefully or that was exactly what he would have.

Grandma Em's chin was thrust out, her eyes sparkling with defiance. Luke nearly laughed out loud as his eyes swung to Christine. She sported the same mulish look, ready for battle. Two against one. It just wasn't fair. Luke knew that another tactic was needed here.

"Who climbed the ladder?" he asked, as if he didn't really care.

"I did."

"Christine." The women answered in unison.

Luke sat and eyed each woman in turn. Both were on the verge of speaking in their own defense when Luke stood.

"Well, ladies, the porch looks nice. You paint very well." This said, Luke bent and kissed Grandma Em's cheek. "Thanks for lunch. I'll see you both Sunday." And with that he left.

You could have heard a feather drop in the kitchen after the front door shut. Neither woman spoke. Feeling shame at how defiantly they had behaved, Emily and Christine exchanged sheepish glances and moved to do the dishes. As Christine worked, she realized that Luke still didn't know how much she appreciated the verses. Feeling double the guilt, she worked on, determined to let Luke know some way on Sunday.

23

With a final look in the mirror that took in a fresh shirt and clean blue jeans, Silas headed down the hall to Luke's room. Luke, having just slipped into his suit jacket, turned to find Silas standing in his bedroom, eyebrows raised in surprise. Luke would have left the room at that time, but Silas wandered in and dropped down on the bed, eyeing his brother with amusement.

"You've already impressed the Chambers family enough to get the horses at a good price. Why the suit?" Before Luke could answer, Silas went on. "It wouldn't have anything to do with the address of one Miss Caroline Chambers I saw on your dresser, would it?"

"I just thought it would be nice to welcome them to Baxter smelling better than a horse." Luke's voice sounded defensive, even to his own ears, and he wasn't sure why. He really didn't expect to see Caroline, let alone encourage her if he did.

Movement below Silas' beard told Luke he was fighting laughter. Silas looked down at himself before asking with feigned innocence, "Do I smell all right? Maybe I should change into a suit too."

This brought a reluctant smile to Luke's face, and his voice was gruff to hide his amusement. "Get to the wagon, Silas, before I leave you home."

Baxter's train station was uncrowded—unusual for a Saturday afternoon, but a blessing nonetheless. The three horses coming in for the Cameron ranch would be ready for a low-key arrival.

Luke and Silas stood together and watched the train pull in. Luke's hand went to the neckline of his shirt when the second person went by and greeted him as Mark. Silas' laughter didn't help. The train had stopped and people were disembarking, so there was no more time to worry about clothing.

Within minutes Frank Chambers was on the platform, his eyes skimming over the station. Luke stepped over to him, Silas at his heels.

"Luke!" Frank Chambers' hand was extended and his smile was friendly.

"Good to see you, Frank. How was the trip?"

"It was fine, just fine."

"Where is Mrs. Chambers?"

"She didn't come. Our niece had her baby, so Lily stayed home to play mother hen." Frank looked his disappointment.

Luke was about to introduce Silas when Caroline stepped from behind her father. "Hello, Luke," she said softly. The look in her eyes was nothing short of worshipful.

Feeling a bit flustered, Luke made the introductions. Caroline barely took time to nod in Silas' direction before her eyes once again clung to Luke. Frank didn't seem to notice. Silas left immediately after that to check on the horses. Frank went with him, leaving Luke and Caroline alone.

"I've missed you, Luke." Caroline's voice was soft and a bit anxious, nervous eyes shining up at him.

Luke only smiled faintly and asked about the luggage. He then bent to lift the large trunk and missed Caroline's face, her disappointment clearly revealed.

Luke hauled the trunk into the wagon before leaving Caroline to assist the men.

Frank had a mare's lead in each hand. Silas was holding the stallion when Luke approached. "You certainly didn't exaggerate, Luke. He's a beauty." Silas' voice more than words spoke his admiration.

Luke smiled and patted the firm neck, speaking softly to the magnificent animal. Titan was black, completely black, from the tip of his proud nose to the end of his long tail. His eyes showed intelligence and spirit. A sound from the mares caught his attention. He answered with a loud snort, sidestepped, and tossed his finely shaped head.

"Let's get this guy home. We'll drop the Chamberses at the hotel and head out."

Some hours later the three horses were settled in their new home, fed and comfortable. As the men headed back to the house, Silas spoke. "I take it you are not headed back into town tonight?"

"How did you know that?"

"Miss Chambers didn't look too happy with you when we left."

"No, she didn't, did she?" Luke replied with a frown. "It was Frank's idea. He said he was beat and that they would see us in the morning. I forgot to tell Grandma Em that there would be two more for dinner tomorrow."

"It won't matter. I'll tell her in the morning."

"*You* will? Where will *I* be?"

"I figured you would go and have breakfast at the hotel with the Chambers'. I can get Gram's chores.

"Oh. Well, thanks for the offer, Si; I'll think on it."

The men had reached the back porch. It was getting cooler, the days shorter. The sun was sinking low.

"What did you think of her?"

"I didn't really get a chance to talk with her." Silas' answer was accompanied by a small shrug. But the look Luke shot him clearly stated that he believed Silas had sidestepped the question.

With a heavy sigh Silas answered, "She seems young."

Luke's face was pensive. "I think so too."

The men fell silent for a time. As the sun dipped behind the trees and hills it cast an orange glow on the Cameron ranch.

Silas stood and stretched. "I'm headed in, but I want to tell you something—something I believe with all my heart. God won't hide His answers from you. If Caroline is the woman God has for you, you'll know. If you continue to trust, He'll continue to be your guide."

These words said, Silas touched Luke's shoulder and went into the house. Alone now, and in deep thought, Luke sat until darkness completely covered the land.

". . . they arrived on the 4:15 yesterday. Luke would like to bring them to dinner."

"Of course the Chamberses can come to lunch. How did the horses do on the trip?"

"They're fine. You'll have to get out and see them. That stallion is a beauty."

"We'll plan on it. Christine, let's go out this week, maybe Thursday or Friday."

"That sounds fine. I'm a little anxious to see the ranch."

Grandma Em and Silas both stopped eating. They stared at Christine and then at each other before speaking, as though they had forgotten she was there.

"I can't believe this, Gram. All these weeks and she hasn't seen the ranch!"

"I feel just awful. I know she'd love it. She told me she misses her own horse. How could we have overlooked such a thing?"

"Ahem!" Christine felt she needed to remind them of her presence.

Grandma Em turned. "That settles it, Christine. We'll go out this week, rain or shine." With a determined nod, Grandma Em went back to her breakfast.

Christine was left to wonder what was so special about the ranch. Her grandfather's stables housed four horses, one being Raven, Christine's own horse—her pride and joy. The thought of seeing the ranch and its horses left Christine in a buoyant mood for church.

Driving into the church yard and being greeted by name felt good to Christine. Mrs. Nolan was in the entryway as usual. She squeezed Christine's hand and said a few words to Silas about her niece Amy.

98

A brief flash from last week went through Christine's mind and she moved quickly to be first in the pew and next to the wall.

Pastor Nolan said he was fighting a cold. He would need to keep things short today because his throat was bothering him. Only one song was sung before the sermon began.

"Today I would like you to turn to First John chapter 4, beginning with verse 7." Pastor Nolan read these verses and began to talk about God's love.

"God is love. The Scriptures tell us this over and over. In John 3:16 we see the greatest expression of this love. Listen as I read John 3:16: 'For God so loved the world that he gave his only begotten Son, that whosoever believeth in him should not perish but have everlasting life.' Who is the only begotten Son in this verse? It's Jesus Christ. He alone is qualified to take on the sins of the world, for He is God. In John 10:30 are Jesus' own words: 'I and my father are one.' "

Christine turned the pages and read John 10:30. A smile lit her face. She knew this verse. It was the first one on the list that Luke had given her. Shifting slightly in her seat, Christine looked past Grandma Em in hopes of catching Luke's eye. She need not have worried—Luke was already looking her way. They exchanged a quick grin before turning their attention back to the sermon.

"All have sinned and come short of the glory of God— Romans 3:23. 'All have sinned,' it says. Maybe you think that's just not true. You might say, 'I've never sinned. I've never stolen from someone or killed anyone. Those are sins and I've never done those.' But the verse says, 'All have sinned and come short of the glory of God.' You see, in the light of God's holiness, we have all sinned. Pride, greed, unforgiveness, gossip—the list is a long one. God will not allow these things into His heaven. Heaven is God's home, and He alone decides who will enter.

"But there is hope. Read on. Romans 3:24 says, 'Being justified freely by his grace through the redemption that is in Christ Jesus.' Jesus Christ is the answer to all your needs." Pastor Nolan stopped and cleared his throat. His voice was getting hoarse, but he continued.

"My throat isn't going to let me go on much longer, but I must ask you this: Do you know where you would spend eternity if you were to die today? God loves you and sent His Son for your sins. My friend, have you ever confessed your sin to God and told Him you believe that Jesus died for those sins? Have you ever opened up your heart to Him? He is waiting for you with open arms. Your prayer need not be complicated or elaborate. The Word says, 'Believe on the Lord Jesus Christ and thou shalt be saved!' Do not put it off, my friend. No one knows how long his time on earth will be. Don't wait! Go to Christ and open your heart to Him. He will gladly enter in. He is your only answer to everlasting life as well as an abundant life here on earth. Do it today!"

The closing hymn was led by Silas. His voice was deep and clear. In his closing prayer, he asked for God's healing hand upon Pastor Nolan and for those who had not yet accepted Christ.

Once back in the wagon, Silas managed the reins, with Grandma Em sitting beside him. Christine slid forward from her place in the backseat until her face nearly touched Grandma Em's shoulder.

"Grandma Em?" Emily shifted around in her seat with an expectant smile on her face. "You told me your husband, Joseph, was on the other side. Did you mean heaven?" At Grandma Em's nod she went on. "He believed in Christ and you think he is in heaven?" Again Emily only nodded. "And you also believe in Christ and believe you're going to see Joseph when you die?"

"With all my heart, Christine."

It was Christine's turn to nod. Placing a cool hand on Christine's flushed cheek, Grandma Em spoke through tears. "I know you are searching, Christine. I also know that God is your answer. God loves you so much, and I'm praying, Christine, that you will open your heart to that love."

Even though the horses were at a crawl, they were already pulling up to Grandma Em's house. Unlike on most Sundays, everyone including Luke and his guests had arrived ahead of Grandma Em, so she decided it was best to let things go for now.

"If you want to talk later, Christine..." she let the sentence go unfinished. Grandma Em hugged Christine and then Silas was helping her from the wagon. Christine watched as she hurried toward the house.

Christine was preoccupied when Silas helped her down from the wagon. So she was doubly surprised when Silas gave her a big hug. The embrace broken, Christine stood staring at him with wide, surprised eyes. It took a moment for her to realize that in Silas' own quiet way he knew she was hurting. A gentle finger came out to touch the end of her nose, and he smiled kindly at her before moving away to take care of the horses.

Reluctant to go inside, Christine's footsteps were weary as she walked to the house. Knowing there was no way she could be alone, Christine made an effort to put her confusing thoughts aside.

Christine had no more stepped into the entryway when a small blonde person ran through the parlor and hid behind her skirt. Within moments Charles was planted in front of Christine, hands on his small hips. "I know you're back there, Em. It's my marble and I want it back."

"Cal gave it to me." The small voice was muffled, and Christine wondered if she were crying.

"He can't give it to you. It's mine."

Christine, who was needed in the kitchen, was on the verge of stepping in when Mac appeared beside his small son.

"I hope you have a good reason for trapping Christine against the front door." John MacDonald dwarfed the five-year-old, but Charles showed no fear as he pointed toward Christine's skirt. "Emily is back there and she's got my marble."

Mac's eyes followed the direction of Charles' finger and laughter rumbled out of his chest when Christine's skirt moved around her legs as she herself stood perfectly still. "Are you harboring a fugitive, Christine?"

"Not intentionally," Christine laughed with him. She made an attempt to move toward the kitchen, but the little girl behind her had other ideas and held fast.

"Go ahead, Christine, I'll get her," Mac said.

Christine turned then and exposed Emily. In one movement, surprisingly fast for a man Mac's size, she was in his arms. Christine glanced back before walking quickly through the house. Charles was standing below his father, looking up at the little girl in his arms. Emily's hand was clenched into a fist, the coveted marble obviously inside. Mac was smiling and saying something to her, but Emily's lower lip was out a city block and she was looking most unreasonable.

Christine entered the kitchen to find everything under control. "When you came through the house, Christine, were the kids getting along? I thought I heard raised voices." Julia spoke from her place at the stove.

Christine peeked at the gravy that Julia was stirring before moving toward Susanne, who was slicing fruit into a bowl. Christine gently removed the knife from Sue's grasp. Taking the smaller woman by the shoulders, she steered her to a chair at the kitchen table. Christine then took over where Sue had left off, all the time explaining about Emily, Charles, Mac, and the marble.

Julia, Grandma Em, and Sue all laughed at the end of the story. Christine joined them, unaware of how much their laughter was over the way she had maneuvered a very pregnant Susanne.

Julia's eyes lingered on Christine as she worked. She was so much a part of them now—just like family. She felt a sting behind her eyes as she silently prayed that Christine would soon be a member of God's family too.

Earlier Grandma Em had quickly told her and Susanne about the conversation in the wagon. Grandma Em had said a quick prayer as they stood together in the kitchen, asking God to save Christine and to use them as instruments as He needed them.

25

Not until it was time to sit down to dinner did Christine meet Frank and Caroline Chambers. It was to date the most humiliating introduction that Christine had ever experienced.

"Christine, this is Frank Chambers. We bought the new horses from his stables in Chicago." Christine shook his hand. "And this is his daughter, Caroline." Christine's hand went out for the expected handshake, but Caroline's words stilled her movements. "Why, you're as tall as Julia!" Caroline's voice was shocked and slightly outraged.

Joseph Bennett had, from the time Christine was small, instilled in her a pride about who and what she was. She had never been allowed to slouch or to be ashamed of her height. She was told to hold her head up and look people in the eye. But at that moment she felt she would have given a year off her life to be a foot shorter.

Christine's eyes took in the petite woman before her: big, light-blue eyes, very blonde hair, pale skin. Christine felt as big as Mac and as dark as the wooden Indian downtown.

Caroline didn't realize how her words sounded, so she went on. "Of course, I shouldn't be surprised, since most all of the Camerons are so tall." Caroline smiled adoringly up at Luke.

"Oh! I'm not related to the Camerons. My last name is Bennett."

"That's right," Luke said, smiling kindly and putting his hand on Christine's shoulder. "Christine lives here and works for my grandmother."

"She works for your grandmother and she's going to sit down to dinner with us?" Caroline's voice was incredulous.

Christine drew back as if she'd been slapped. Caroline's words had been spoken without thought. Watching Luke and Christine exchange a smile in church, plus watching him put his hand on her shoulder, had been fine—until she found out they were not related to each other.

Slowly Caroline became aware of a tense silence which had permeated the room. Even her father, who thought she could do no wrong, was staring at her as if she had taken leave of her senses.

Surprisingly enough, Christine was the one to save the meal. Quietly and with a calmness she herself could hardly believe, she said, "Let's eat."

For Christine the meal was a strain. She ate mechanically. The food that had smelled so good in the kitchen now tasted like sawdust in her mouth. As the meal progressed, Christine's embarrassment faded to an emotion she could not quite define. Something almost painful stirred within her each time she saw Caroline's hand on Luke's arm and each time she leaned toward him to smile into his face. What Christine failed to notice was that Luke's return smile was forced and that he had glanced in her direction more than once to see how she was faring.

But, no, Christine didn't see any of this. She only saw a pretty blonde who made her feel ungainly, too tan, and unwanted. Plus this intruder had Luke's full attention. So Christine continued to eat, feeling miserable and every bit as green as the color of her eyes. It might have helped to define the word, but Christine, having never before been jealous, was left in the dark. Her thoughts were bleak, even going so far as preferring Spooner with all its danger to being in Baxter today.

"Did anyone see you come?"

"No, sir, no one."

Vince Jeffers grunted and glared at the man before speaking. "Get back to the Bennett house."

"What for?" The small man interrupted.

"Just shut up and I'll tell you." Vince growled at the man. "I think the old lady has heard from the girl. Look for a letter, a paper with an address, anything that would lead to wherever she's hiding." Vince Jeffers' voice lowered to a deadly calm before continuing. "You'd better not mess up this time. I'm nearing the end of my patience. Now get out of here and don't return until you have an address for me."

Long after the hired man left, Vince sat in the shadowy study. Time was running out. Already he had lost out on two deals requiring large sums of money he simply didn't have.

Rising, he went to the window. Winter was nearly upon them. The days as well as his time continued to shorten. He didn't know if he could take another winter in Wisconsin, but without that money he was going nowhere.

Vince's words echoed in the stillness of the room with deadly self-assurance. "I'll find you, Christine Bennett, and when I do, you'll pay for the trouble you've caused me before you die."

26

A loud snort sent a white mist billowing into the crisp morning air as Luke's mount tossed his head and pawed the earth. They had ridden hard, Luke giving the horse his head, willing to follow his lead.

Now the horse stood atop a small rise. Luke was still mounted and surveying the Cameron ranch. The setting was peaceful, and Luke's heart swelled with thanksgiving for the wealth that he and Silas shared—not money (although they never went hungry) but the land, its heritage, loved ones, health, the fine animals they bred. He could have gone on forever.

An hour earlier, when Luke had saddled Titan, his thoughts had not been so peaceful. Not for a moment had his mind been off Caroline and her thoughtless words that had hurt Christine. Luke's emotions had run the gamut: anger, frustration, pity, despair, compassion.

Sunday Luke had waged an inner battle over speaking with Caroline. But it was taken out of his hands on the way back to the hotel. Frank had rebuked Caroline in front of Luke, and, whether out of embarrassment or true belief that she had done no wrong, Caroline had stomped into the hotel without a word of apology. Frank had expressed his own regrets before going into the hotel with a worried frown on his face.

Normally Luke would have put the entire affair in the back of his mind, feeling it was Frank's to handle. But the fact was that the Chamberses were his guests, and he felt responsible.

He would never forget the look on Christine's face; she didn't deserve that kind of treatment. She worked hard and was honest. Luke respected her.

Heeling Titan into a smooth gallop, Luke reflected on his previous time in prayer. He had put all these feelings at

Christ's feet and had come away knowing that God's hand was at work. His heart had been settled about Caroline and he had petitioned God from the bottom of his heart about his emotions. Fervently asking God to keep the compassion he felt for Christine from turning into a stronger emotion, he knew that Christine's salvation was the most important goal right now.

With these thoughts settled in his mind, Luke went up to the house for breakfast, still thanking God for whatever His work was to be.

27

Coughing into her apron, Christine squinted against the dust billowing around her. She hated beating rugs. There had been a time as a little girl when she couldn't wait to help Mrs. Hall with her work, but even then beating rugs had been miserable. She couldn't get it done fast enough.

Grandma Em had walked downtown to the post office and to run errands. Christine worked desperately to get finished before she returned.

— ⁘ —

Luke rushed into the livery stable. If he didn't hurry, he would be late arriving at the hotel and lunch with the Chamberses. He tugged at his necktie and prayed for patience. Dressing up for the third day in a row was not his preference. A quick check with Jack about the leather harness to be ordered and he could be on his way.

Jack was bent over a horse's hoof. Luke was standing quietly waiting when he felt a tap on his shoulder. He looked up to see the sheriff beckoning to him and moving a few stalls away. Luke stopped beside the man and nearly spoke when the sheriff said in a quiet voice, "I've heard from the sheriff in Spooner. He's a good man whose reputation precedes him, and I trust him." Luke opened his mouth to ask the sheriff what he was talking about, but the man went on. "He sent a description of Maxwell, the missing man, and has several leads he plans to check out. He'll keep me informed. It's up to you what you share with Miss Bennett, but I thought I'd let you know." With a tip of his hat, the man was gone.

Luke stood frozen, feeling as if someone had just thrown a hard right punch to his stomach. His thoughts were in chaos. The sheriff in Spooner, a missing man, Miss Bennett, Christine?

Stumbling out of the livery, the harness and lunch with the Chamberses forgotten, Luke headed to his brother's house. Somehow he knew Mark had the answers to his questions, and Luke had every intention of getting them.

— ✣ —

"You got a letter!" Grandma Em called up the stairs. Christine came rushing down, an excited smile on her face. She remembered her manners just before tearing open the envelope. "How was your walk into town?" she inquired politely.

Emily laughed merrily, shook her head, and walked toward the kitchen. "Open your letter, Christine. We'll talk later."

Christine did as she was bade, her hands shaking.

Dear Christie,

I miss you. The house is empty without your smiles and laughter to warm the day.

The weather is getting cold now. The sheriff said it would be too conspicuous to send a box, so I ordered you a coat. Write me when it arrives.

I realize, Christie, it's hard for you not to be here. I will go through your grandfather's things and treat everything with the utmost care.

The Sheriff also told me to send word to the sheriff in Baxter. I'll send news as I receive it. The search for Carl Maxwell goes on.

Please take care of yourself, Christie. My heart and thoughts are with you.

Love,

Mrs. Hall

Christine folded the letter and put it in her pocket. A tear slid down her cheek. Carl Maxwell was still missing. He might even be dead. A shiver ran down Christine's spine as she thought of death. If Carl was dead, would she be next? The thought rode hard upon her that day and even into the night.

— ✜ —

With a final fist into his pillow, Luke gave up on getting comfortable. Sleep was as far away as the North Pole.

Stabbed! Mark said Christine had been stabbed. Luke's heart wrenched at the thought. His eyes closed and he was once again in Mark's office.

"So you see, I didn't have a chance to tell the sheriff he had the wrong brother. I'll ask you again, Mark. Why is the sheriff in Spooner interested in Christine?"

Mark's battle with his oath was short. His brother's question was from the heart and born out of a fear for his grandmother, Christine, and the entire family. So Mark quietly told him all he knew, beginning with the night he carried Christine into his office and ending with the talk under the willow tree last week.

Luke sat in stunned silence as he listened to all that Christine had suffered in complete innocence. He was in full agreement with Mark: Her arrival in Baxter was no coincidence. God had put her here to find Him.

Luke rose from the bed. The room was chilly, but he didn't notice the cold as he pulled a chair near the window and sat looking at the crescent moon.

Caroline's anger at his being late to the hotel drifted momentarily across his mind before his heart stepped before God. Luke claimed every verse he knew about God's love and salvation for the lost. He placed Christine in God's hands with each verse, unaware of how desperately his prayers were needed at that very moment.

— ✜ —

"No! No!" Christine's screams rent the air. Her door slammed open just as Grandma Em stepped into the hall.

Christine rushed toward the stairs but stopped short at seeing Grandma Em. "He's trying to kill me! I've got to get away. He's got a knife!" Christine's voice was high-pitched and hysterical, her eyes like saucers as she gestured wildly before racing again toward the stairs.

"Christine!" Grandma Em reached for her but Christine eluded her grasp. "Christine!" Grandma Em followed her down the stairs, silently pleading with God for help. "Christine, it was just another dream. Christine—please stop."

Nearly to the parlor, Christine in her haste missed the last step. She fell forward, her head hitting the wall to the side of the staircase before she rolled onto her side and lay in a heap at the bottom.

She sat up and rubbed her head in confusion. Grandma Em knelt beside her, her face lined with worry. Christine's eyes went back up the staircase. It was coming back to her in a rush: She had had another nightmare.

Would she ever get over her fear of death? She was so far from Spooner but still haunted by her fears. She felt helpless. Tears filled her eyes and she began to tremble. "I'm sorry," she choked out.

"Shhh, don't cry. It's all right. I'm right here." Grandma Em's hand smoothed Christine's tumbled hair and gently touched her cheek. "Let's go back upstairs."

Christine was still trembling as she sat on the side of her bed. Grandma Em sat beside her, listening and praying. "He was by my bed at home. He had a knife. I thought it was real and he was right here in the room with me."

"Christine." Something in Grandma Em's voice pulled her out of her miserable shell and made her look up. "Christine, what if you had died tonight, if it hadn't been a dream and you were really killed?" Emily let this sink in for a moment. "Where, Christine? Where would you spend eternity?" Grandma Em's voice ended on an urgent note.

"I don't know," Christine whispered in confusion and misery.

"Were you listening on Sunday, Christine? Did you understand what Pastor Nolan said? Believe on the Lord Jesus Christ and you shall be saved."

"I've never prayed before. I don't know what to do." Christine's voice was slightly breathless. It was coming again, that feeling of expectancy that overtook her whenever she went to church or heard Bible verses.

"Believe, Christine, only believe," Grandma Em said gently. "Pray and tell God that you know of your sins and that you believe Jesus died for them. Trust in Him now, Christine, for your eternal salvation and His loving care for you now here on earth."

Christine sat still for a moment as she felt the wonder of Grandma Em's words bubbling up within her. It was all so clear now—her searching, her fear. God was waiting to take them all—waiting for her, Christine Bennett, to hand them over to Him.

Bowing her head, Christine began to pray. "Dear God, I believe in Your Son, Jesus Christ, and that He died for my sins." Christine's voice broke as she struggled to bring her tears under control. "Thank You, God, for coming into my life. Amen."

Christine turned and looked at Grandma Em, but neither woman could see through the tears that flowed unchecked. Neither woman could speak or find a handkerchief, so the silence was broken by sniffs and small sobs with an occasional breathless laugh.

Christine drew in a shuddering breath. "I have so many questions."

Grandma Em squeezed her hand. "Will they wait till morning?"

Christine smiled and nodded her head. The women embraced and Grandma Em made her way back to her room. Her head barely hit the pillow before she fell into the most peaceful sleep she had known since Christine had arrived. Down the hall Christine's eyes were also closing. Her plans to lie awake and talk to God melted as sleep claimed her with a smile on her face.

28

Emily stood at the door of Christine's room. Taking in the made bed, she saw that all else was in place and quiet. She had expected Christine to sleep late. After putting the coffee on, she peeked out and saw Christine coming toward the house.

"Good morning," Grandma Em called as she opened the door. Christine hurried toward her, a smile lighting her face.

"Good morning, Grandma Em."

"How are you, Christine?"

"I feel wonderful. You, on the other hand, are probably ready to boot me out of the house for all the nights' sleep I've cost you."

Grandma Em's answer was quite serious. "Having you find Christ, Christine, has been worth every moment."

Christine's answering smile was serene. "It feels peaceful and wonderful knowing that God loves me so much. I'm sure you understand how lonely I was after losing my grandfather."

"I know, dear. The hurt can feel as though it's going to overwhelm you. But I promise you this, Christine: God is bigger than any hurt you'll ever have." It felt wonderful having Grandma Em to share with, Christine thought as the two women readied breakfast.

That morning during Grandma Em's reading and prayer time Christine prayed too. It was simple and heartfelt and was followed by questions from Christine which took all morning. "If the Bible is God's Word, why was it written by men? How do you know God is everywhere at once?" Christine never seemed to run out of them, and by lunchtime Grandma Em was exhausted.

After they had eaten, Grandma Em went to her room for a nap. Luke and Silas came into the kitchen just as Christine was finishing the dishes.

"Well, hello!"

"Hello, yourself!" Silas answered as he leaned against the dry sink. Luke took a chair at the table.

"Where's Gram?" The question came from Luke. He had prayed so much last night, in ignorance about Christine and Grandma Em, that he felt a bit concerned for them today.

"She's upstairs taking a nap."

"She's not sick, is she?"

"No, no, just tired."

"And you, Christine, are you okay?" Luke asked, but both men had noticed the high color in her cheeks and the almost-fever brightness in her eyes.

"I'm fine. In fact, I'm wonderful. Last night I accepted Christ into my heart." Christine's smile was beaming.

Luke's eyes closed against a sudden rush of tears, his hands tightly clenched in his lap. He felt as if his heart would burst through his chest, so full was his joy.

Silas let out a yell and laughed as he grabbed Christine in a hug that threatened to break her back. Setting her down, he gave her a hearty kiss on her cheek and she joined in his laughter.

Luke had risen from the table and was headed toward Christine. She suddenly felt shy. Luke stopped before her but didn't touch her. The expression on his face was tender and understanding, and when Christine's eyes met his, she blushed furiously.

Silas felt immense happiness that he wasn't attracted to this girl. The only time he had ever seen her blush was in front of Luke. Silas wondered if Luke was aware of it.

Luke, upon seeing the blush, smiled and said quietly, "I prayed for you last night."

"You did?" Christine hoped her voice didn't sound as high-pitched to his ears as it did to her own.

"I'll tell you about it sometime."

"Okay," Christine answered, feeling oddly breathless.

"A woman my age needs peace and quiet for her afternoon naps." A falsely indignant voice spoke from the kitchen doorway. Everyone laughed, and what followed was a chaotic time of excitement and questions, smiles and rejoicing.

Before the day was out, the entire Cameron family knew of Christine's decision. Pastor Nolan also heard. He and Mrs. Nolan came by to talk with Christine and Grandma Em after supper.

Christine fell into bed that night exhausted and overjoyed. As she lay quietly talking with God, she prayed for all the trouble and goings-on in Spooner without being specific. She asked for special protection over Mrs. Hall and a safe end for everyone included in this turmoil. Christine placed her fears and worries in God's hands and fell asleep peaceful and trusting.

— ✦ —

"Baxter?" Vince Jeffers looked once again at the paper in his hand: "c/o Emily Cameron, Baxter, Wisconsin."

"Is this all there was?"

"I think so. The old lady started to stir around and I had to get out of her room."

"You went all the way into her bedroom?" Jeffers' voice was incredulous.

"I had to—that's where her desk is," the small man defended himself.

"Were there other papers—a letter, perhaps?"

"Mighta been a letter, but since I can't read to tell..."

Vince Jeffers for once was not angry; he looked thoughtful. "Something tells me we've found her." He spoke as he poured each man a liberal helping of brandy. "Sit down. We've got some planning to do."

29

"Hurry, Daddy, I can't wait to see Luke's ranch," Caroline stated.

"What's your hurry? The ranch isn't going anywhere."

At her father's answer Caroline turned with a huff on the buggy seat. This action brought a grimace of pain to her face.

"Can you believe this buggy? It's ancient and this seat is like a board, and to top it off, it was the best the livery had!" Caroline's voice was heavy with disgust.

Frank slanted a look at his daughter, thinking as he did so how he had courted her mother in a buggy worse off than this one. At the time he didn't have two nickels to rub together. But it hadn't mattered; he and Lily, then and still today, had eyes only for each other.

Before Caroline came along, Frank had taken over his father-in-law's breeding yards. By the time Caroline was four he was well-established, his reputation was spotless, and his stock had more than tripled.

Caroline, too young to remember anything except a fancy house with many servants, had never worked a day in her life. Frank knew it was his own fault that she was more little girl than woman. When his little girl had begged to come north with him in Lily's absence, he couldn't say no.

But he was brought out of his reverie by his daughter's whining. "Are we almost there?"

The road rounded a large clump of trees, and, just as Luke had directed, the house was in view. With an eighth of a mile Frank was turning up the driveway and pulling the buggy to a stop in front of the house.

Silas came out the front door just as Frank helped Caroline down from the buggy. "Hello!" he greeted them with a friendly smile. "Luke is in the barn. Come on, I'll show you."

The three of them made their way around to the side yard and headed for the massive, well-built structure housing the Camerons' 26 horses. They found Luke in the alleyway between the stalls, checking the injured foreleg of a four-week-old colt. The colt's mother beckoned to him from a few stalls away, giving Luke the extra chore of trying to hold the young animal still.

Without a word Silas stepped over to hold the colt's head, freeing both of Luke's hands for the leg.

Frank stood still, admiring the two men as they worked gently and effectively with the horse, unaware that the train of his daughter's thoughts was quite different. Dressed in her yellow riding habit, she expected to catch Luke's eye the moment she walked into the stable. She felt angry at his lack of attention. She determined to make Luke notice her today so he would want to see her every day they were here for the next few weeks.

The Chamberses stayed long at the ranch that day. The cool weather was perfect for riding, and they spent most of the afternoon on horseback.

It was "during supper that Frank announced that he and Caroline would be going home Monday. Caroline's reaction told Luke and Silas that she had not known.

"Monday? But we just got here! Why Monday?" Caroline whined and argued, but Frank was adamant. "I'm ready to get home, Caroline. You understand, don't you, Luke?"

"Of course, Frank."

"I'll be back sometime when Lily can come. She would love your rolling hills."

"You'll be welcome anytime," Luke assured him.

Caroline proceeded to pout through the remainder of the evening. Luke, unaccustomed to this in a grown woman, felt he needed to make amends. The way Caroline's face lit up when he asked her to go riding with him Saturday morning told him he had been duped. Realizing it was too late now, and feeling disgust at his own gullibility, he had a date to go riding with a spoiled young woman whether he liked it or not.

— ✣ —

Christine shifted once again before leaving her seat to pace around the room. She turned to find Grandma Em watching her. "I feel so excited about seeing the ranch tomorrow. I can't sit still. What time will we be leaving?"

Grandma Em laughed as she answered. "Right after breakfast so you won't have long to wait." The women talked for awhile before Christine retired early, somehow hoping to make morning come sooner.

Knocking and then pounding at the front door awoke Christine. The pocket watch on her bedside table said 3:45. Christine heard Grandma Em's bedroom door open as she reached the parlor. Upon opening the front door she found Maggie with Emily in her arms, wrapped snugly in a quilt, dead to the world.

Grandma Em appeared as Maggie stepped into the entryway. She transferred her bundle to Christine before speaking. "Sue's pains started around midnight. Her water broke about an hour ago and things are moving pretty fast. The Doc thought it would be best if Emily woke up over here."

"Thanks, Maggie," Grandma Em said; "give them both our love and tell them we're praying." After Maggie left, Grandma Em led the way back up the stairs with a lamp in her hand. When she moved toward the spare bedroom, Christine's voice quietly stopped her. "Grandma Em, can I take her into my bed?"

"Oh, Christine, you don't have to do that. She's slept in here before."

"I know I don't have to, but I want to." Christine snuggled the little girl closer to her. "She's precious, isn't she?"

"Yes, she certainly is. You go ahead and take her to your bed. I'll see you both in the morning."

Wrapped inside the quilt along with Emily was needed clothing for the next day. Christine hung the little dress in her own closet before easing into bed beside a still-sleeping Emily.

As was becoming her habit, Christine prayed before she slept. Tonight she pulled Emily close beside her and asked God for a child of her own.

30

"How many pancakes have you eaten?"

"I think five."

"Five! My goodness, you're going to pop!" This brought gales of laughter from Christine's small charge. Christine couldn't think of when she had had more fun. Emily had thoroughly captured her heart.

They started the dishes together. Emily was on a stool, a drying towel in her hand and teaching Christine a song, when Grandma Em called from the parlor. "Emily, your dad is here."

Squealing, Emily jumped down from the stool and headed through the door, with Christine right behind her. Emily threw herself into Mark's arms. Father and daughter hugged for awhile before Mark took a seat. Emily sat in his lap with an anxious Christine and Grandma Em on the couch across from them.

Mark looked both tired and happy. Grandma Em had asked no more than if everyone was all right, knowing that Mark wanted to share with Emily first. He was careful to talk directly to his daughter, even though he could feel Christine and his grandmother's eyes on him.

"Emily, do you know why you're over here this morning?"

"Yes, 'cause Mama's having our baby."

"That's right. You have a brand-new baby sister."

Mark watched Emily's face as she comprehended his words. Her eyes widened before she asked, "The baby's already here?"

"She's here."

"Can I play with her?" This question brought laughter from the adults. Mark stopped when Emily tugged on his shirt. "What's her name?"

"Her name is Elizabeth. Elizabeth May Cameron." Mark's voice held contentment and pride.

"My name is Emily Susanne Cameron." Emily's voice was stubborn and her lower lip trembled just a bit. Mark immediately recognized the signs of jealousy and lifted Emily until they were nearly nose to nose. "I know that's your name. I remember the day you were born and named you after your Great Grandma Em. And right now Elizabeth is the most blessed little girl in all the world to have a big sister as wonderful as you."

The words were exactly what Emily needed to hear. She gave Mark a hug that threatened to cut off his air before scrambling down from her father's lap and announcing she was off to see Mr. Turley. The back door slammed and she was gone.

"How's Sue?"

"She's good, Gram. Things went much faster this time. Maggie, of course, is incredible. I could have used her when Emily was born."

"Elizabeth is such a beautiful name. What time was she born?"

"Just before 5:00. What time do you think you'll be over?" Mark stood. "I've got to get word to the ranch and Julia."

"Why don't we keep Emily another night and come over midmorning tomorrow? We were headed to the ranch this week, but that can wait. Maybe when you and Julia go riding on Saturday, Christine, you could stop out there."

"That's fine. Anything to keep Emily another night."

Christine smiled at Mark. "She slept with me last night."

"Did she hog the bed?"

"No, with this cool weather we just cuddled up together in the middle."

"Well, I can't thank you enough, and I'll see you tomorrow."

The next 24 hours went by in a rush. Emily helped Christine with all her work, including the feeding of the stock. It took twice as long to get everything done, but it was also twice the fun. By the time they were walking over to see the baby Elizabeth, she, and Christine were fast friends.

Grandma Em and Christine sat in the living room while Mark carried Emily upstairs to see her baby sister for the first time. About ten minutes passed before Mark came partway down the stairs and called to them.

Sue was in bed, sitting up against the headboard. Beside her was Emily, looking proud and holding a tiny bundle in her lap. The women approached the side of the bed. Upon seeing her newest great-granddaughter, Grandma Em began to cry.

Christine didn't cry, but stood in wonder at the tiny person before her. Sue's eyes went to Mark at the foot of the bed. They exchanged a warm look at Christine's reaction.

"Emily, can Christine hold our new baby?" her mother asked softly.

"Oh no!" Christine exclaimed loudly, making Elizabeth start. Quietly now, "I'm sorry. I didn't mean to frighten her."

"She's fine—she'll have to get used to noise if she's going to survive around here," Sue assured her.

Emily spoke from her place on the bed: "This is my baby Eliza, Christine.

It was Christine's turn to cry, and her voice sounded choked through tears. "Oh, Emily, your baby Eliza is beautiful!" Emily began to get squirmy, so Mark rescued his youngest daughter. Holding her, he turned to Christine. "You're welcome to hold her."

Christine shook her head no. Elizabeth was so new and helpless-looking against Mark's chest.

"How about Great-Grandma?" Mark asked with a smile.

Grandma Em, still sniffing, replied, "Let me dry up a bit and I'll sit down and hold her."

Some 20 minutes later Elizabeth began to fuss and Sue looked tired. Mother and daughter were left alone.

Downstairs, Maggie and Christine prepared lunch. Right after they ate, Julia showed up with the boys. She and Mark hugged for long moments, brother and sister sharing in this special event together.

Joseph Cameron Sr. had delivered Calvin, but Mark and Julia were recalling the night Mark had delivered Charles. Susanne, his nurse then and not his wife, had assisted. Mark had commented aloud as he held his minutes-old nephew, his eyes a bit wet, "The only thing better would be to deliver one of my own." As Mark said these words, his eyes locked with Susanne's, the room and its occupants fading from sight as this young doctor and nurse regarded each other, their hearts in their eyes. Julia found out later that Mark had asked Sue to marry him that very night.

Arriving very late back at Mark's office to clean up, Mark had cornered Sue in the equipment room.

"I saw something in your eyes tonight and I want an explanation."

Sue, painfully shy at that time, had tried to step past him, but he would have none of it.

"Move out of my way, Dr. Cameron," she had ordered as firmly as possible, her heart pounding in her chest.

"Not until you tell me," he stated quietly. She could see he was not going to budge.

"All right," she cried, "I'll tell you. I did exactly what you told me not to do after you hired me: I've fallen in love with you. But you need not worry that I'll be a problem, Dr. Cameron, because I'm leaving first thing in the morning." This painful admission out, Sue buried her face in her hands and burst into tears.

Mark's arms had come out and gently pulled her against his chest. Remembering the day a few weeks after she had arrived when he had uttered these words, Mark was disgusted. What conceit! He saw now that he had said them as a defense against the attraction he felt for her immediately upon seeing her, an attraction he fought as it grew daily.

Mark had pulled out his handkerchief as Sue's crying subsided. He gently dried her tears before bending his head and tenderly brushing her lips with his own. A declaration of love fell easily from his lips and came straight from his heart. Sitting in his office, they had talked until sunup.

The next day a beaming Mark and radiant Sue had announced to the family that they would be married.

Now, five years later, the family did a little reminiscing. Christine was all ears when Julia began to question Mark about the birth, the water breaking, the time spent pushing, etc.

Remembering the night when Raven was born, Christine spoke without thinking. "It's a little like when a horse foals." This statement brought complete silence—and then uproarious laughter. Christine's embarrassment was saved by Charles, who was quite interested in the idea of a horse having a baby—something he had never witnessed but wanted to. He began to question her. The adults in the room were more than a little surprised at her knowledge. Grandma Em questioned Christine on her experience.

"We didn't live right in town," Christine explained, "so there were no children or young people nearby. When I first came to live with my grandfather, his stables were full—about 15 horses. When I was ten he first allowed me to watch the births. By the time I was 12 I was assisting, but then Grandfather had begun to sell out. Without friends near, seeing them only at school, horses became my world.

"I never told him, but it was torture every time he sold another horse. It had always been just a hobby with him, and he said that when a hobby gets to be more headache than fun, it's time to call it a day. By the time I was 16 we were down to three mares, one of which was pregnant. I helped when Gypsy gave birth to a perfect little mare. Had it been a stallion he would have sold it, but it was a mare so Grandfather gave her to me." Christine fell silent then, a bit appalled at the way she had shared so much of her past.

Christine would have been horrified if she could have seen the wheels turning inside the heads of the three adults seated across from her. It was as if the lights had come on: Christine was a new Christian and she had just shared with them her knowledge of horses. There were two unmarried men in the family who ran a breeding ranch!

Julia went upstairs to see Sue and the baby. Mark had a call to make, and Grandma Em took the children to the front room for a story. Christine rose to help Maggie with the dishes, unaware of the new development in everyone's mind. Christine didn't stand a chance!

31

"Aren't they a bit tight?" Christine stood in front of the full-length mirror in Mac and Julia's bedroom, scrutinizing her jeans-encased legs.

As she pulled on a boot Julia answered, "Maybe a little. But with no one around to see us, I wouldn't worry about it."

Christine shook her head, her voice rueful. "Even if someone does see us, it's better than riding in a skirt!"

"Oh, I heartily agree. My brother thinks I'm rebellious, but he's never worn a riding habit."

"How does Mac feel about pants?"

"If I go right over to the ranch and back, I can go alone. If not, I have to ride with someone and stay on MacDonald or Cameron land."

Once mounted and ready to go, Julia knew a moment's pricking in her conscience. She knew she had stretched the truth, but she shoved her guilt aside, not wanting to spoil the day.

Christine and Julia moved past the MacDonald cornfields, ready for the harvest. They rode in silence, taking in the beauty around them. The horses' sturdy legs ate up the acres as the crisp October air surrounded them.

The fall days brought cool mornings and brisk nights, but by ten in the morning the sun was warming things up to a comfortable temperature that didn't call for sweaters or coats.

Julia pulled her horse atop a small mound and Christine followed suit. Below them sat the Cameron ranch. The house was a single-story rectangle about a hundred feet from the stable, a low-ceilinged structure set at the edge of a well-built corral area.

Christine's eyes took in the horse barn. It seemed enormous to her. "How many horses do they have?"

"I think the three that just arrived made it 26, but the stables will hold well over 30."

Julia sat still for a spell, letting Christine take in the beauty of the ranch setting. After they turned their horses away, Julia led them down along the creek. They let the animals rest and graze, each woman taking a rock and getting comfortable in the morning sun.

"How did you meet Mac?" Christine asked. For the first time in her life the relationships between men and women weighed heavily on her mind.

"He came to the ranch to see my father. Well, actually, it was the first time I had seen him in many years. He had left home when I was still quite young. But when Mac's dad got sick, he came home to work the farm. I was only 13 but already showing signs of being tall, and Mac was so big and acted so grown-up.

"He was 18 at the time, and very kind. He never told me to get lost like Luke and Silas did." Julia laughed softly. "I used to lie awake at night and think about him. Because of his size, I would dream he would come and take me away and then beat up my brothers when they were mean."

Christine laughed at this before asking, "When did he first notice you, I mean..." she grew flustered and silent.

"You mean as a woman."

At Christine's nod, Julia continued. "The summer I turned 15 I had gone into town one day to shop. Mac was in the store and we talked. Later he walked my things out to the wagon for me, and I swear I was head over heels in love. That night after supper he came to call. We sat on the porch and laughed and talked for over an hour. By the time he left I was sure I was in love."

"After Mac left, my father told me I couldn't see him socially again. I remember crying and crying.

"But why, Julia?" Christine's voice was aghast.

"Oh, Christine—I'm sorry. I forget sometimes that you weren't raised around here. Mac and his family were not Christians," Julia explained gently. "And the Bible is very clear on its guidelines for a Christian courting or marrying a non-Christian."

A week ago Christine would have been angry at such a statement. But now she realized it was another of God's truths she needed to learn.

"I best finish the story. I obeyed my father and told Mac I couldn't see him and why. It nearly broke my heart when he accused me of thinking I was too good for him. I didn't see him for quite a few months after that, but I prayed every day that he would trust Christ and understand why I had to obey my father.

"I didn't know until much later that while he had been away, working in the South on a plantation, the plantation owner's daughter used him. She flirted with him and made promises she had no intention of keeping before she up and married another plantation owner's son. She told Mac after the wedding that he would never have been good enough for her. He was very bitter, to say the least." Julia's voice was sad with remembered pain.

"But he did eventually get saved." Christine broke through her friend's melancholy.

Julia beamed at her. "Yes, he was saved. About six months later he came to church. He sat in the back and didn't talk to anyone. It went on like that for some time. Then my father did something that surprised us all—he asked Mac to Sunday dinner. After that the pattern changed. Mac would sit with us, come to dinner after church, and stay until near dusk.

"It was one of those Sunday afternoons when Mac was over that he and Paul, who was only 13 at the time, were talking on the back porch. Paul went over the plan of salvation with him, prayed with him, and helped lead him to the Lord.

"It wasn't long after that my father died. I don't know what I would have done without Mac at that time. He was there for all of us. Less than a year later his own father died.

It was a rough time, but we grew closer to God and to each other because of it.

"Mac asked my grandfather for my hand when I was 17. Grandpa said yes but that he wanted us to wait until I turned 18. So we were married in the fall of 1879, eight years ago this month."

Julia's eyes were filled with tears, her wonder at God's goodness not at all dimmed after all these years.

Christine, caught up in the miracle of Mac and Julia's courtship, asked, "Do you think, Julia, that God has someone for me?" Her voice was wistful, her eyes also filling with tears.

"Oh, Christine, I don't know exactly what God has for you, but I promise it will be wonderful!" They embraced, cried, and talked nonstop for the next hour. The sun was high and Christine's stomach growled, or else they might have been there all day.

— ✤ —

"Do you plan to expand anytime soon, Luke?"

"Expand?" Luke's questioning gaze swung to Caroline.

"Well, yes, I simply assumed with all this land you would be building more stables and adding to your stock."

"Silas and I have no plans at this time to add on," he told her patiently. "We're about to our limit as to what we can handle ourselves."

"Oh, but you just need to hire some help . . ." she was off again. It was as if she hadn't heard a word he had said. Luke was beginning to wonder if the morning would ever end.

For being a horseman's daughter, Caroline didn't ride very well. She was too busy trying to keep her riding habit in perfect order. Straighten here, brush off there. And that hat! It was a useless little number that caused her to keep her head at an odd angle in order to ensure that the hat was in the exact place she wanted.

They had been out for nearly two hours, and as yet Caroline had not stopped talking or giving advice. Luke was getting hungry and his patience was wearing thin.

Caroline was so busy explaining about the way her father had built up with additional stables and help (evidently forgetting Luke had been there) that she failed to notice the two other riders moving in the direction of the Mac-Donald farm.

Without conscious thought Luke adjusted his direction and speed. Caroline innocently followed his lead, talking all the while. "Why, a man from Europe came to see Father's horses. His reputation is flawless, you know." The sound of approaching hooves finally put a halt to Caroline's chatter.

"Hello!" Julia called a greeting as the four riders came together in a small circle.

"You ride in blue jeans?" Caroline's voice was outraged.

Undaunted, Julia just smiled and said, "Oh, Caroline, it's unbelievably comfortable, and we didn't expect to see anyone." Julia's eyes took in Caroline's slightly rumpled appearance, her hat a bit askew and rather dusty.

Christine only saw the flawlessly-made blue riding habit and how it accentuated Caroline's blonde hair and blue eyes.

Luke, on the other hand, had completely forgotten there was a Caroline Chambers. Julia and Christine had raced away from the creek. Julia's pins had held, but Christine's hair, thicker and falling past her waist, had pulled free. It moved with the breeze gently around her face and shoulders. Luke could only stare.

Christine at that moment became aware of Luke's perusal. She made an attempt to bring a little control to her hair, but without pins it did little good. She gave up and let it go. Christine felt her cheeks grow warm under his steady regard, even as a tiny feeling of pleasure began to stir within her.

Luke sat there feeling hypocritical. All these years he

had objected to Julia in pants on horseback, and here he was thinking that Christine looked beautiful.

In all fairness to Julia, he knew she was careful of where she rode, and often Mac was with her. She and Christine would not have seen anyone today if Luke hadn't maneuvered it.

It occurred to Luke just then why Mac never protested to Julia about her riding astride: He liked the way his wife looked in pants. *His wife.* The words seemed to echo loudly in his ears until Julia spoke.

"Have you seen our new niece, Luke?"

He smiled, "Last night."

"Isn't she precious?"

"She is that," Luke agreed with her. "What do you think of her, Christine?"

"I think she's beautiful." Luke's breath caught at the smile on Christine's face when she thought of the baby.

"You were in town last night and didn't stop at the hotel?" Caroline's stringent voice cut through the air like a knife. A brief moment of uncomfortable silence ensued before Julia spoke.

"Well, we're starved and headed for home. We'll see you tomorrow." Luke and Caroline watched them ride away.

In a rare moment of maturity, Caroline watched Luke as his eyes followed Christine's departure. It became crystal clear just then: Luke Cameron was not the man for her. Never once had he hung on her every word the way the boys back home did. And the look in his eyes when he had seen Christine today! Caroline had to admit to herself that she wouldn't know what to do if Luke ever looked at her with that same intensity.

The couple returned to the ranch in silence, Luke feeling regretful. It was never his intent to hurt Caroline. He wished he had known how to handle things better.

Caroline, knowing she had made a fool of herself one too many times, also kept silent.

32

"Mama's back! Mama's back!" Charles' cry was excited and it brought Mac out of the barn.

Both of Julia's sons hung onto her legs after she dismounted and bent to kiss them.

Christine, in watching the little boys at Julia's legs, missed the tenseness that passed between husband and wife.

Once in the barn, Christine moved to unsaddle her horse for a rubdown, but Mac stepped in. "Here, Christine, I'll get that. Boys, take Christine out and show her the puppies."

Christine had no time to protest as each little boy grabbed a hand and dragged her outside.

Julia could feel Mac's eyes resting upon her. She stopped her work and met his eyes over the dividing wall between the stalls. "I'm sorry, Mac."

"Why, Julia? We have an agreement. Why did you break it?"

"I wanted to be alone with Christine so she would feel free to open up with me."

"The boys and I were gone all morning. You could have talked here at the house."

"But she loves to go riding. I thought it would be relaxing for her and she would want to talk."

"Those are all excuses, Julia, and well you know it!" Mac's voice was stern but not angry. "Does Christine know you broke our agreement?"

"I lied to her." Julia began to cry. "I told her I had to ride with someone if I went further than the ranch, and not specifically with you or one of my brothers. I'm sorry, Mac, so sorry. I don't know what I was thinking. I'm sorry!" Julia was engulfed in Mac's embrace, his arms holding her tightly against him.

"I've got to talk with her," Julia hiccuped. "I've got to tell her I was wrong and ask her forgiveness. You forgive me, don't you, Mac?"

"You know I do." The words came out just as he covered Julia's lips with his own.

This was the scene that Christine, Charles, and Calvin came upon when they returned to the barn. Christine held back, but the boys, evidently accustomed to such sights, ran directly to their parents. Mac and Julia each bent to scoop up a child, the four of them sharing a family hug.

Julia broke away and came toward Christine. Upon seeing the wetness on her cheeks, Christine became concerned.

"Julia?"

"We'll talk later," she assured her with a smile. "Come on, we'll change clothes and get lunch on the table."

The MacDonald kitchen was small but cheery. Christine listened with a bit of awe as first Charles and then Calvin thanked God for the meal. To know Christ at such a young age was wonderful.

The conversation around the table turned to the topic of the weather.

"We'll have snow next month, won't we?" Calvin asked.

"I don't know, Cal. It's getting colder every day, but there's no sign of snow." Mac answered.

"Well, it's got to snow in November," Charles stated.

"Why is that?" his mother wanted to know.

"Mama! You can't have Thanksgiving without snow! How would you go sledding?" His young voice was incredulous, as if he couldn't believe his mother didn't understand such important details. The adults all hid amused smiles at this declaration.

After the meal the boys begged Christine to swing with them. Christine hesitated, but Mac spoke his encouragement. "Go ahead. I'll help Julia with the dishes."

Later, as they washed, Mac looked out at the three at play. "Christine looks enough like you to be a sister."

"Considering her face and figure, I'll take that as a compliment, but today I don't believe Luke was thinking of her as a sister."

Mac became instantly alert, his hands going still on the cup he was drying. "Julia, are you matchmaking?"

"No." His wife turned to him with wide, innocent eyes. But Mac looked skeptical. "Honest, I haven't said a word." Mac only shook his head in resignation and went on drying.

Julia watched out the window a moment. "I must admit, I did think of what a good-looking couple they would make, but I wasn't going to say anything."

"Just remember, the Holy Spirit doesn't need your help." Mac felt the need to remind his well-meaning wife.

Julia watched again as Christine pushed first Charles and then Calvin. All three were laughing. The boys shouted at the air as they swung up higher and higher.

Julia sighed. "They would have made such a cute couple. It seems so romantic."

Quietly, so quietly that Julia almost missed it, Mac said, "I think so too."

Julia looked over to see her husband taking special pains with the dish he was drying. Julia moved until she was standing directly in front of him, her height allowing her to look directly up into his face. Mac finished with the dish and reached for another, but Julia's hand stayed him. "Did you picture Luke and Christine together as a couple?"

"It did cross my mind," he reluctantly admitted.

Julia stood there until their eyes met and they both began to laugh. Throwing her arms around his neck, Julia said, "I love you, John MacDonald."

"And I love you, Julia MacDonald."

Once again Christine came upon the embracing couple. This time without the boys, she withdrew quietly to give them privacy.

Moving through the house, Christine went into the parlor and took a comfortable chair. Seeing this happy Christian family caused Christine to feel discontented.

Unbidden, Luke on horseback, handsome and masculine, flashed through her mind. She shoved the picture aside as she also saw Caroline, lovely and dainty in her blue riding habit, on the horse beside him.

Christine was still praying for she knew not what when Julia joined her. "I really should be getting back to Grandma Em's."

It was tempting for Julia to simply agree to this and take Christine back, but she knew it was best to get it out right now.

"I wanted to talk to you before you go." Christine, remembering Julia's tears in the barn, waited quietly. "I did something wrong this morning, Christine, and I need to tell you and ask your forgiveness."

Christine's eyes widened but she kept her peace. "Earlier I told you when I rode further than the ranch I needed to go with someone. I was not completely honest. My agreement with Mac is that I ride with either him or one of my brothers." Julia stopped, her eyes on the clenched hands in her lap, too ashamed to even look at Christine.

"You're my new sister in Christ. And instead of being an example and a help to you, I lied to make myself look important and to impress you. I would ask you, Christine, from the bottom of my heart, for your forgiveness."

"It's all right, Julia..."

"No." Julia cut her off. "Christine, it's not all right and I don't want you to say that it is. Saying it's okay would be condoning what I did. Saying you forgive me would tell me you understood I've done wrong, but you accept my apology and we can forget it and go on. Can you forgive me, Christine?"

Christine saw the truth and importance in Julia's words and was thankful for them. She took Julia's hands in her own. "I forgive you, Julia. I love you and thank you for coming to me. You *have* been a wonderful example to me today. More than you'll ever know."

"Thank you, Christine. I couldn't have asked God for a more special friend."

All four MacDonalds took Christine home that afternoon and stayed to share a light supper with her and Grandma Em. Mac, Julia, Charles, and Calvin hugged Christine as they left, thinking that their lives were a bit sweeter with the presence of Christine Bennett.

33

Since it was too soon for Sue and the baby to be out, Sunday dinner was at their home. Sue stayed up in bed, allowing one visitor at a time, but Elizabeth was brought downstairs and she made the rounds.

The table space at Mark and Sue's did not allow all the adults to eat in the dining room. Christine cheerfully agreed to eat in the kitchen with the children. Luke scowled in Christine's direction as she headed for the kitchen. He was unaware that her reason for going to the kitchen was because she genuinely loved spending time with the children and not because of Caroline's remark the week before. He thought about going after her, but decided against it.

Christine saw the frown and wondered at it. It stayed with her even as she enjoyed a wonderful time with the kids. The three children tried to outdo one another on memory verses. Christine was amazed at all they knew.

Finally she asked, "Why do you memorize Bible verses?"

Calvin answered, "It helps you not to sin. There's even a verse about it." The children all thought for awhile, but could not remember it.

Luke, standing unobserved at the doorway, came in and whispered in Emily's ear. She beamed at them and said, "I will hide God's Word in my heart." She hesitated, and Luke again bent to her ear. Emily nodded and started over. "I will hide God's Word in my heart that I might not sin against thee." Luke kissed her cheek before pulling up a chair at the table.

Suddenly Christine lost her appetite, so conscious was she of Luke's presence right across the table. She listened to him and the children but only sipped her milk and pushed her food around for something to do with her hands.

"Aren't you going to eat? You can't have dessert unless your plate is clean. Don't you like chicken?" Emily's innocent questions set Christine's cheeks ablaze. She looked over at the little girl next to her and then back at her plate, knowing that the table was quiet, awaiting her answer.

Christine wished with all her heart at this second that the floor would open up so she could fall through.

"Have you always embarrassed so easily?"

Christine's head snapped up at this casual question to find Luke regarding her thoughtfully, his elbow on the table and his chin propped up in his hand. Christine's blush only deepened as he studied her face.

"Uncle Luke, you shouldn't tease Christine." Calvin, who knew his uncle well enough to have caught the teasing tone in his voice, admonished him in a grown-up way.

"You're right, Cal," Luke answered, all teasing gone and without taking his eyes from Christine's face, "but Christine is beautiful when she blushes. It's nearly impossible to resist." Luke smiled at her then. Perfect white teeth stood out against his tan features.

He continued to smile and regard her with such warm amusement that Christine couldn't stay at the table. Luke, who half expected her to give as good as she got, felt badly when, too flustered to speak, Christine fled the table and began to prepare water for the dishes.

Luke sat a bit longer with the children. He noted how Christine was careful to keep her back to the room. Her every movement spoke of tenseness, and he knew that saying anything, even in kindness, would only make matters worse. So, taking pity on her, he left the kitchen.

"How long have you been a nurse, Maggie?"

"Ah! Now that would be telling. You might even be able to guess my age." As usual, Maggie was businesslike.

Christine laughed and said, "It must have been wonderful to see Elizabeth come into the world."

"You're right about that. In all my years of nursing it's a sight I never grow tired of."

"Are you the only person in your family in medicine?"

"No, no, my father was a doctor and my oldest brother has a practice. His daughter, my niece, is in nurse's training right now. So you can see that my decision to become a nurse was an easy one."

"Well, for purely selfish reasons I'm glad you are," Christine told her.

Maggie laughed, "Let's get this coffee to the front room."

Christine carried a tray full of cups and saucers. Maggie's tray held the coffee, cream, and sugar. Christine's idea to help Maggie serve went out the window when, after she set her tray down, she noticed the occupants of the couch.

Luke sat comfortably holding his baby niece, her downy blonde head moving, her eyes open and searching as Luke talked to her. Next to him, leaning over his arm to see the baby, was Caroline. The entire pose was so tender and familylike that Christine felt tears beginning to form.

Mumbling an excuse to no one in particular about checking on the children, Christine turned for the back door. Once outside, Christine drew in great gulps of cold air, somehow hoping to freeze the ache in her chest. She could hear the children at the side of the house and took a quick peek to see if they had their sweaters on. Christine thought absently of the coat that Mrs. Hall had ordered. She would be needing it soon.

Christine strolled around the backyard, noticing that the remnants of Sue's vegetable garden looked lonely and cold. Lonely and cold—the way Christine had begun to think of Spooner. The thought of leaving Baxter made her want to cry. "Not Baxter," Christine told herself, "but the people." How could she leave these people? The thought hurt. But if she were honest, it would be easier to go than stay and see Luke and Caroline get married. Christine was shocked at the anguish it caused her to think of this prospect.

"You've done it now, Christine Bennett." Christine's voice broke quietly through the cold air to her ears alone. "You've fallen in love with a man who is interested in another woman. You're going to be hurt and it's no one's fault but your own."

Wanting nothing more than to sit down, feel sorry for herself, and have a good cry, Christine knew she had to get her mind off Luke and Caroline.

Grandma Em had once said that God is bigger than any hurt we might have. Christine prayed as she went around the house to play with the kids, "Please, Lord, be bigger than this hurt that threatens to overwhelm me. Help me to trust You for my future and accept Your will for my life."

34

Luke stood on the platform until the train was completely out of sight. The sound no longer echoed in his ears, and the vibration beneath his feet was now still.

The send-off had been easier than he had hoped. Caroline had been reserved but not sullen. Frank had praised him for his stables and the fine work he and Silas did. He had promised to try and get up next spring if the Missus could come.

Luke knew he had some things to get done at the ranch, but if he hurried to the post office he would be able to squeeze in a trip to see his grandmother, not once admitting, even to himself, whom he really hoped to meet.

His horse tied out front, Luke opened the door for a woman carrying a box so big it nearly obscured her. A muffled thank you came from somewhere beneath the box as the woman moved out the door and a few steps past. Luke suddenly realized who it was.

Large hands on Christine's shoulders brought her to a surprised halt. Before she could turn, those same hands reached around and lifted her box up and over the top of her head.

Even as Christine turned, some sense told her it was going to be Luke.

"Good morning, Christine."

"Good morning," Christine answered and reached for her box. Luke let it go.

"How are you today?" Luke again took the box from her grasp.

"I'm fine. What brings" you to town?" The box was once more in Christine's hold.

"I was seeing the Chamberses off." The way he had casually stated seeing his girlfriend off, as if he didn't care, made Christine angry, and when Luke reached to take the box again she stated firmly, "I can carry it myself. It's not heavy." Had Luke known her better, he would have realized that her temper was coming to the fore. She had realized he had been flirting with her at the table yesterday, only to go in and sit cozily with Caroline on the couch. That night in bed Christine had made a decision to stay away from Luke Cameron as much as possible until it was time for her to go home. Now, running into him the next morning was almost more than she could take.

Luke, thinking to keep things light, said exactly the wrong thing. "I don't know about where you come from, but around here a gentleman helps a lady with her packages."

Christine, believing he was playing false with Caroline in the pretense of being a gentleman, let her temper boil over. "I do not need *you*, of all people, to remind me of the social amenities, Mr. Cameron," Christine gritted out icily between clenched teeth.

Luke was stunned. What in the world had he done to anger her?

Christine, taking advantage of his silence, said, "Good day, Mr. Cameron," and turned on her heel.

Christine seethed all the way home. Her long stride eating up the blocks, she walked and saw nothing. People waved at her but she missed them. The box grew heavy but she gave it little notice. "What nerve!" she fumed. "Put his girl on the train one minute and forget she exists the next. What a flirt!"

Christine stomped up the porch steps. Letting the box slide down until it landed at her feet, she reached for the handle, but the door opened before her hand could make contact.

To her utter surprise, Luke reached out and took her box under one arm. With his free hand he pulled her inside.

The door shut firmly and he spoke. "I will know, Christine, before I leave here, why you are angry."

The two faced each other in Grandma Em's parlor. Christine's surprise at seeing him did not diminish her anger. Her voice was heavy with sarcasm. "Did you have a nice visit with Caroline, Luke? It must have been hard to put her on the train and say goodbye. I imagine you'll miss her very much." Christine's eyes spoke her disappointment and hurt.

Luke finally understood. Her anger was a cover for the hurt she felt.

"Christine, there is no commitment between Caroline and me."

Christine looked confused before she asked, "Does Caroline know that?" thinking back to the adoration she saw in her eyes.

"She didn't when she first arrived, but she does now."

Christine couldn't look at Luke. How many times was she going to make a fool of herself in front of this man? Her eyes took in the carpet with great interest as she spoke. "I'm sorry I was angry at you. I have a nasty temper."

"You have a temper? I didn't know that!" There it was again. That supremely innocent voice and expression that told Christine he was having one on her. To her amazement, she didn't blush.

"I really am sorry," she repeated, now able to look him in the eyes.

He was sensitive to her serious tone. "I'm sorry too, Christine. There was no way you could have known there is nothing between Caroline and me." Or that my interest is right here in this room, he added silently to himself.

"Thank you for explaining to me. Considering it's really none of my business, that was kind of you."

"Aren't you a little curious about what's in the box?" Luke was ready to change the subject.

"Oh, it's a coat." At Luke's questioning look, she explained, "Mrs. Hall, a friend of mine at home, wrote that she ordered it for me."

"Aren't you going to at least look at it?" Luke asked, wondering, and then thinking better of it, if he should tell her he knew she was from Spooner and who Mrs. Hall was.

When the box gave her trouble, Luke slipped a small knife free from his front pocket and with a few cuts had the box open.

Christine's hands moved the wrapping aside until she spotted a bit of white. Without thinking, she pulled, and out came a lace-trimmed cotton camisole that she held at arm's length.

"I wonder if there's been a mistake." Christine looked over at Luke, who was standing beside her. His eyes took a short glide over the very feminine garment before saying to Christine, "If that's the heaviest thing you're going to wear this winter, you're going to be cold."

With a gasp Christine realized what she had been standing there holding for his inspection. Quickly she shoved it back into the box. She should have known Mrs. Hall would order more than just a coat, especially since it was such a big box.

Christine couldn't keep the stammer from her voice as she attempted to right the box to carry it upstairs. "It would really make a mess—I mean the box. I should open the rest later—well, that is, in my room." When she realized how she sounded, she stopped and said, "I have to go now." With that she grabbed the box and ran quickly up the stairs.

Grandma Em came in some minutes later to find Luke in the exact spot that Christine had left him, simply staring at the place where Christine had been standing.

"Luke, is everything all right?"

He turned absently to his grandmother. "Did you say something, Gram?"

"I said, is everything all right?"

A beaming smile broke across Luke's face. "Everything is just wonderful, Gram." Grandma Em watched him walk to the door, whistling a little tune. He gave her a small wave before exiting.

Emily shook her head as she went to find Christine. "I wonder if there has ever been a case history of spring fever this close to November."

35

November began much like October, but by halfway through the month the temperatures had dropped. Luke rose one morning to find that the fire had gone out in the kitchen stove. Blowing into his hands, Luke stomped around for warmth before attempting to light the fire.

When the fire was stoked and the coffee on, Silas came out, barefoot and shivering. He and Luke huddled near the stove, waiting for the coffee to become drinkable.

"Why don't you get married so we've got someone here to take care of us?"

To this long-standing joke between the brothers Luke answered as expected: "If I did get married, the first morning she got a look at that furry face of yours she'd go screaming from the house and we'd be alone again."

Silas was a sight first thing in the morning. His dark, thick hair stuck out in all directions. His beard, usually brushed down in some semblance of order, was in riotous disarray. Luke said he looked like a grizzly bear.

Two cups of coffee later, both men were warmly dressed and headed for the stables. They worked together feeding the 26 horses.

"Gram and Christine will be coming out to the ranch Friday morning," Silas commented offhandedly.

"They will?" Christine's name snared Luke's complete attention.

"They were supposed to come a few weeks ago, but with Elizabeth's birth and Emily staying with them, it just didn't work out. I'll be going to get them midmorning."

"Don't you have a buyer coming Friday morning?"

"Yeah, but I'll have time."

"I'll go for you."

"It's cold, Luke—I couldn't ask you to do that," Silas answered with his face averted, and it took Luke some minutes to realize he was being teased.

"Am I that obvious?"

"Not to anyone else. You forget I live with you." The men finished up in silence and went to the house for breakfast. Silas was a great cook, but this morning Luke's attention was elsewhere.

He finally spoke. "Si, are you and Christine more than friends? I mean, are you interested in her?" Luke wasn't sure why he had asked, but the thought came to him in the stable and he couldn't quite shake it.

"If you're trying to ask me if I'm in love with Christine, the answer is no." Silas leveled a look on his brother. "Are you in love with her?"

"I don't know. I'm attracted to her—I have to admit that. I was attracted to her before she got saved. I did a lot of praying in an effort to keep my feelings in obedience. I think it was almost a relief to have her be saved so I could relax when I was around her. Now being able to relax around her has just increased the attraction."

"How do you think she feels about you?"

"I think she's scared to death of me. I was barely able to exchange two words with her Sunday."

"Calvin told me she cried because you teased her."

"She cried?" Luke's voice was alarmed.

"It was the Sunday we ate dinner at Mark and Sue's. Calvin said when she came out to play with them, her eyes were wet and that earlier you had teased her at the table."

Luke was looking miserable. Were the tears because he had teased her or because she thought he was committed to Caroline?

"Luke, why don't you go see her this afternoon? Go and stay for supper. Tell her you're looking forward to her coming Friday. Next week is Thanksgiving. We'll all be together the entire day. If there's a strain between you two, you'll both be miserable. Go see her. Talk to her."

Christine pulled the pie from the oven. It smelled wonderful. "I wonder if Luke likes apple pie. Stop it, Christine!" she told herself in frustration, wishing she had a nickel for every time she had thought of him today. As close as it was to afternoon chore time, she would be a rich woman.

Keeping busy had always kept Christine's mind off her troubles, but not so where Luke Cameron was concerned. When she was sweeping she remembered the warm way he smiled at her. When she ironed she remembered the warmth of his hand, lightly and briefly on her back so she could precede him out of the door of the church.

Time between Sundays was long, and when at last the next Sunday came, Christine determined to make the best of it. But when Luke had complimented her dress, and innocently asked if it had come with the new coat, Christine was so painfully reminded of the scene with the camisole that she didn't even answer him.

She hadn't said ten intelligent words to the man. He probably thought her addlepated!

Christine scolded herself. "You, Christine Bennett, are not getting paid to daydream!" A quick peek at her roast and she had to get to the barn.

"Grandma Em, I'm headed out to feed!"

"Okay," Grandma Em's voice answered from somewhere upstairs.

Christine tugged on the ancient overcoat she used for her barn chores and slipped out the back door.

Luke took his brother's words to heart. He finished his work and was back in the house by 3:30 for a shave and a bath. Silas kindly saddled a mount and Luke was on his way to town by 4:00.

He rode at an easy pace, allowing his mind to work on the feelings he had for Christine. He would never have been so presumptuous as to assume that God had placed Christine in Baxter and saved her just to give him a wife. But maybe God did have something special for the two of them.

Luke praised God daily for Christine's salvation and her interest in Christian growth. Grandma Em had told him that she and Christine studied together nearly every morning, and that Christine was an avid student.

Luke asked himself if he loved Christine. He just wasn't sure. Loving was risky business. His parents and grandfather had been most dear to him. It had not been the same relationship as husband and wife, but it was a painful loss nonetheless.

He was not worried that Christine was going to die, but she did live in Spooner. There was nothing stopping him from going to see her there, but the idea of not having her in Baxter really bothered him. He wanted a chance to get to know her and was not quite sure how to go about it.

If he found he loved her and she didn't return that love, the rejection would be bitter. On the other hand, if she fell in love with him and his feelings were not that strong, she would be hurt. Luke rebelled strongly against this idea. She had been hurt by too many people, and he was determined not to be one of them.

Luke had just arrived in town when he really began to listen to himself. He wasn't trusting God at all. He was worrying and fretting about something over which God had complete control.

Luke began to pray silently, his heart humbled before his heavenly Father. He confessed the pride he had felt when thinking he could deal with this issue without God's help.

A special peace stole over Luke as he communed with God. He asked God's help in obeying His will, come what may, and in listening to his own heart about Christine. Luke remembered what Silas had said: God won't hide His answers. If God wanted Luke and Christine together, Luke would eventually know it.

36

The first hit of cold air took her breath away as Christine stepped from the warmth of the kitchen. She shivered a little as she walked to the barn. The door was kept closed in this weather, and when Christine got inside she lit a lamp to see.

"How's my sweet old Caesar tonight?" Christine said affectionately to this faithful old friend as she fed him. "Are you keeping warm out here? I'm afraid it's going to get much colder before we see spring." Christine stopped talking abruptly and stood still a moment. She thought she smelled smoke. Figuring it was from someone's stove, she went back to work with a shrug.

"You're going to get fat and lazy..." her words died off.

She *did* smell smoke. But where? Not until Christine stepped completely out of Caesar's stall did she see the cause.

The barn was on fire, over by the door. Christine did not panic but ran toward the blaze, stripping off her coat as she hurried.

With the coat she began to beat at the flames, but they were spreading quickly out of control. Feeling the heat on her face, Christine knew she had to get out.

The animals! Quickly Christine ran to Chester's stall. He had been strangely quiet tonight, Christine thought absently as she grabbed the scruff of his neck and began to pull. She knew opening the door would fan the flames, but she had no choice.

Throwing the door open, Christine ran out into the cold. Taking deep breaths of fresh air, she left Chester some ten feet away before running back to the barn.

Hesitating at the door, Christine could see that the flames had multiplied in those few seconds. Taking the hem of her skirt, she covered her face and charged back in.

"Please, God," she prayed, "please let Caesar come willingly," knowing how fearful horses were of fire.

Once in the stall, Christine grabbed his halter and tried to move him. He tossed his head, his nostrils dilating as he inhaled the smoke. Trying to resist her, his eyes rolled fearfully in their sockets.

Thinking that an eternity of breathing smoke and praying had passed, Christine miraculously felt the horse back out of the stall.

"Thank You, God," she sobbed as she looked toward the barn door. The leaping flames made their passageway to safety small, but Christine determined to get Caesar out of the barn or die trying.

Caesar fought Christine as she pulled him along the alley between the stalls. Quickly losing visibility, Christine tried to coax him along with words, but her voice was choked off by the smoke.

The smoke nearly blinding them now, Christine began to feel dizzy and lightheaded. She felt her way along the stalls, silently pleading with God for strength.

Amazingly, the door was in sight! Fresh air! They were going to make it! Caesar picked that time to lunge for the door, knocking Christine against the wall. She felt the flames burn her ankle and calf. A quick turn and she was through the door, only to trip on the threshold. She put her hands out as the ground came rushing up to meet her, but suddenly strong arms were surrounding her, lifting her high against a solid chest.

Christine squinted up through painfully dry and burning eyes to see the clean cut of Luke's jawline above her. He looked down then, his features sharp with concern and then softening with tenderness as his eyes met hers.

It was the *tenderness* she saw there amid all the places she hurt. Turning her soot-blackened face into his coat and clinging with all her might, Christine began to sob.

She was still clinging to Luke and crying when she felt the softness of a mattress beneath her back. Luke laid her gently on her own bed and stayed bent over her. He realized, prior to this night, that he had never known the meaning of the word "fear."

Upon arriving and seeing the smoke, Luke had run to the backyard. His grandmother had just come out of the house and called to him that Christine was in the barn. Luke had thought his heart was going to stop.

"Luke?" Christine croaked in a dry cough.

"Shhh, don't try to talk. Gram sent a neighbor for Mark."

"The animals?"

"The animals are fine. Now, not another word."

"Please don't leave me." Again another cough seized her.

"Shhh," he said as he gently placed a finger on her dry lips. "I'm right here, I won't leave you." Luke attempted then to straighten away from the bed, but Christine grabbed frantically for him. He bent over her once again. "I'm just getting out of this coat. I'll be right here." Her eyes slid closed at his comforting words and she wondered if she had imagined the kiss she felt on her brow.

It could have been a minute or an hour later—Christine could not gauge—when she felt someone pulling her shoes off.

"Luke?"

"Luke is in the hall. He hasn't left you. Maggie and I are here to take care of you. When we're done, Luke can come back in." Mark's reassuring voice came from somewhere above her.

Christine lay still after that, only protesting when her ankle was touched. Gentle hands washed her and helped her into a soft, fresh-smelling nightgown. When a glass was held to her lips, she drank without question. The door opened and she heard Mark's voice. "You haven't much time before the powder does its job." Before Christine could work through these cryptic words, Luke was back beside the bed.

Easing down on the bed beside her, Luke watched as Christine focused in on his face and smiled. Luke smiled back as he placed a hand on either side of her, knowing the medicine was taking effect.

Christine reached to the face above her and touched Luke's cheek. Her smile broadened when she realized he was really there.

"I'm here," he said softly. Christine's hand dropped to the front of his shirt, where she grabbed a fistful of material and hung on. "I have to go to sleep now." Her voice was slurred and she made no move to release him.

"All right, I'll see you in the morning."

Her eyes slid shut and Luke sat quietly a moment before Christine's eyes flew open again.

"Luke?"

"I'm still here."

"Do you like apple pie?"

"It's my favorite," he answered in bemusement, wondering what had brought this on.

Her eyes closing again, Christine let out a huge sigh. Luke sat with her long after her breathing evened out and the hand holding his shirt fell slack against her side. Luke found it hard to breathe when he thought of how close he had come to losing her. You didn't withhold your love from a person just because it might be risky. This was clear to him now.

"She'll be fine, Luke." Mark's voice spoke from the foot of the bed.

"What if she wakes in the night and calls for me?"

Luke loved the fact that she wanted him there. And soon he would tell her just how much he wanted to be there.

"Maggie is staying in the guest room just in case she wakes up, but it's not likely. She'll sleep through the night and you can come back in the morning. Your losing a night's sleep is not going to help anyone."

Luke nodded reluctantly and Mark moved toward the door.

Luke turned down the lamp until the room was bathed in a soft glow. Christine's head on the pillow was turned toward Luke. His eyes moved a final time over her lovely face. He bent and kissed her cheek. "Good night, Christie." Luke's words came softly as he sat, almost in wonder over the realization of the love he felt in his heart for this woman.

37

For the second time in not many months, Christine awoke to find Maggie nearby. Gone was the fear of the unknown, replaced this time with just a calm security at seeing her familiar face.

Maggie helped Christine drink a glass of water and then left to tell Mark his patient was awake.

Within minutes both Mark and Maggie were at her side. Christine, still drowsy, lay quiet as Mark checked her leg. It was tender and, he told her, not badly burned. As Christine began to come fully awake, many questions were coming to mind. Mark pulled the desk chair up to the head of the bed and sat down.

"Your leg looks good. The only thing I'm concerned with is your nose, throat, and lungs. You took in a lot of smoke, and I want you to stay in bed until I give you leave to get up. And no talking!"

"No talking?" Christine croaked, thinking of all the questions she had.

"Does your throat hurt?"

Christine knew what he was getting at and stubbornly refused to answer.

"Christine!" Mark's voice was very stern, and he sounded amazingly like Luke. "Does your throat hurt?"

Her jaw set, Christine gave him a short nod.

"Until it stops hurting, you are not to talk."

"How am I to communicate?" Tears sprang to Christine's eyes, born of a sore throat and frustration.

Mark answered with his best bedside manner. "There will be someone here to check on you at all times." She watched Mark produce a small pad of paper and a pencil from his pocket. "If you can't answer with a nod or shake of your head..." Mark tapped the pad and put it on the bedside table.

Christine was on the verge of telling Mark to take his orders and get out of her room, but she began to grow weary and she ached all over. Suddenly the fight went out of her and her eyes closed, not wanting to fight sleep or anything else.

Mark took Christine's sleep as a peaceful acceptance of her situation. Unaware of how far this was from the truth, he headed out to see what Mac and his brothers were finding.

— ✛ —

Mark found Mac, Luke, and Silas, along with a few other neighbors, looking around the charred remains of the barn. There was talk of possible causes for the fire. The family was thanking the men who had carried water and soaked the ground surrounding the barn, seeing that the structure itself was going too quickly to be saved. It had been a small barn, and thankfully the closest building was well over a hundred feet away. But the water surrounding the barn had been an extra safety precaution.

When Luke found a moment with Mark, he asked about Christine.

"Her leg is in good shape but I think she's feeling pretty weak. She was asleep when I left her."

"She sounded so hoarse last night. Will her throat be okay?"

"I've told her to be quiet until her sore throat is gone, but I think she'll be fine. She wasn't too happy with the idea of not talking."

"Telling a woman not to talk is like saying 'sic 'em' to a hound dog." Both men laughed at this and started toward the house.

Close to an hour later, with everyone just finishing breakfast, Maggie came down to prepare a tray for Christine.

Christine, wrapped warmly in her robe, was sitting up in bed brushing her hair. She could hear voices downstairs and wondered what was happening.

Christine reached for her Bible but didn't open it. She leaned her head back against the oak headboard and began to pray. Christine told God what an awful patient she was. She was rarely sick, and when she was, she made herself miserable by fretting about things not getting done until she could be up and around again. She and Grandma Em worked so well together. Christine asked God to soon put her back on her feet so she could be of help again. Christine's prayer was interrupted when the questions she had had earlier that morning began to roll once again through her mind. They destroyed her peace and made her feel weary. Did the barn burn down completely? Where were the animals? Who was taking care of them? Did anything else burn? Was anyone hurt? Tears again filled Christine's eyes as in frustration she asked God to help her obtain some answers.

She was feeling sleepy again, and try as she might she couldn't stop herself from drifting off.

Less than five minutes passed before Luke came through Christine's door bearing a breakfast tray and a smile, only to find her sound asleep. She had scooted down a bit and was curled against her propped-up pillow. Luke adjusted the pillow and covered her with the bedclothes, as Christine continued to sleep. He wondered if he would get to see her at all today.

As it turned out, he did not. When Maggie reported that she slept through lunch and on into the afternoon, Luke knew he had to get home. So with a final check on her he made his way home, hoping that tomorrow she would feel up to company.

38

Grandma Em's hands joined Christine's as she briskly rubbed her wet hair with a towel.

"We're both going to be in trouble when Mark finds out about this. If Joseph were alive, he'd take me to task."

Christine opened her mouth to speak, but Grandma Em dropped the towel over her face. "I know, I know, your hair smelled like smoke and you couldn't stand it. There. Now, can you sit up for a bit longer?" Christine nodded. "Good, we'll brush your hair out while you sit in this patch of sunlight in front of the window."

As Grandma Em brushed, she talked. Knowing that Christine was concerned about the animals, she started with them. "Caesar and Chester are fine. They're both out at Mac and Julia's. Belle and Betsy are at Mr. Turley's. And the hens I'm afraid didn't make it." Christine turned to look at Grandma Em, but she only patted Christine's shoulder and went on. "The barn burned completely down, but nothing else was damaged and you were the only one hurt."

The look Christine threw at Grandma Em told her she felt she was fine, but Grandma Em only ignored her. A few more strokes and she was done.

"Okay, back into bed. How about some lunch?"

"Gram!" A man's voice sounded at the bottom of the stairs.

"It's Luke. We're in trouble now," Grandma Em said before she left the room.

"How's Christine? Can I go up and see her?" Luke spoke before his grandmother even hit the landing.

"She is much better. In fact, she was up this morning."

"You mean she was out of bed? Why was she out of bed?"

"I'll let her tell you—I'm going to fix lunch." Grandma Em went to the kitchen feeling like a coward.

Once upstairs, Luke knocked on the open door jamb and walked into Christine's room. She was sitting up in bed, looking content with a book in her hand. Christine watched as Luke took in the wet towels, hairbrush, and chair near the window. Next his eyes went to Christine's hair, still unbound and a little damp, falling in soft waves around her shoulders.

Luke's voice was calm and measured. "You got out of bed today against Mark's orders in order to wash your hair?" Christine nodded calmly.

"Why?"

Christine wrote and handed Luke the pad.

"It smelled like smoke?" Again, the calm nod. "You washed your hair because you didn't like the smell of smoke?" When Christine didn't answer but only looked at him, Luke opened up to a rare show of temper.

"That's ridiculous. Absolute foolishness. It's freezing outside and it's cold in these upstairs rooms. You had no business getting out of this bed." Luke ranted on, but Christine had tuned him out and reached for the pad. She handed Luke one sheet of paper and smiled when he sputtered to a halt.

"Hush up, Luke," he finally read out loud, his voice incredulous.

The two eyed each other for endless seconds before Luke spoke more to himself but still aloud. "How did your grandfather control you?"

"He didn't try." Even though her voice was hoarse, Luke caught the underlying steel in her tone. He turned then and walked from the room, leaving Christine to wonder if he would ever be back.

Luke sat down at the kitchen table with a heavy sigh. "You shouldn't have shouted at her," Grandma Em began.

"She deserves more than to be shouted at."

"No, Luke, she doesn't."

"You sound as if you agree with her getting out of bed."

"I helped her wash her hair."

"Why, Gram?" Luke asked in total bemusement.

Emily sat at the table with him. "Luke, try to see things from her standpoint. She slept yesterday away. She had had no news about the barn or the animals you know she cares for. The smell of her hair and sheets was making her sick to her stomach. She also feels much better, and I for one could not see standing on ceremony and waiting to ask Mark. So I grumbled at her and got her washed and back into bed as quickly as I could."

"How do you know all of this?"

"She had written me quite a long letter full of questions and frustration. She was standing next to my bed when I woke this morning so she could deliver it personally. I told her Mark would not like it, but she was determined and I could not say no.

"I hope, Luke, that you won't let your pride punish both of you. Christine and I talked for some time this morning about why God would let this happen. I know it was hard for her not to have an answer land in her lap. She's also feeling good enough to be bored. If you are not going to stay, please go by Julia's and tell her Christine needs company."

Again, Grandma Em went back to the tray she was preparing to bring upstairs. She delivered it and then returned to the kitchen to get lunch for Luke and herself. Luke made the mistake of not returning to Christine's room until after lunch. He would find out the hard way that when Christine was left upset and alone with her thoughts, they moved like wildfire and usually in the wrong direction.

"He had no right shouting at me," Christine told herself. "I am not answerable to him. If I want to wash my hair when I feel good enough to do so, it's none of his business. How would he like to smell like smoke?" This was the train of Christine's thoughts as she picked at her lunch. It had been easier than she expected to not talk; her throat *did* hurt.

Her leg throbbed some, like a sunburn, but other than that she felt pretty good.

So with all these thoughts in mind Christine made a decision. As soon as she was on her feet, she would take the train home. She didn't see any problem in being home by Thanksgiving.

"Hello," Luke said as he came through the doorway. Christine politely set her lunch aside and watched as he pulled her desk chair around and straddled it. Even in her irritation that he had come back when once again she had decided she had made a mistake about him, she couldn't help but notice how he spilled over the chair. It was so rare to find someone who could make her feel small and protected. It was getting harder to hold onto her anger as she remembered those arms holding her, his presence when she needed him most.

Luke could see she was angry with him. He felt he should apologize for shouting at her and should tell her his anger stemmed from the fear she would get sick, that he cared too much about her to want that to happen. Not knowing how to start, he said, "Silas told me you were to come to the ranch tomorrow."

Christine nodded.

"I was thinking we could change your visit to next week, the day after Thanksgiving. Would you still like to come?"

Christine reached for her paper. When Luke saw her answer was longer than a simple yes or no, he felt a sinking sense of dread. He read the paper she handed to him. "I'm sorry I won't get to see your ranch, but I'm going home next week. Thank you anyway."

"Home?" Christine nodded. "To Spooner?" When her eyes turned wide with surprise, Luke said, "Yes, Christine, I know you're from Spooner. The sheriff mistook me one day for Mark and told me some things. I went to Mark immediately and demanded that he tell me the entire story."

"You're very good at demanding things, aren't you?" Christine's voice was icy.

"Yes, I can be very demanding, just as you can be extremely stubborn," Luke answered her.

Christine turned her head away from him in anger and looked out the window. She heard his chair move and, assuming he was leaving, was surprised when he moved it up to the head of her bed and leaned close to her.

Christine wouldn't look at him. Luke waited patiently, and when she still didn't turn he reached and took one of her hands in both of his.

This brought her head around as she looked first at the way his hands swallowed her own, then up into those deep blue eyes glued to her own.

She looked confused, but she didn't pull her hand away, and Luke was encouraged. When he spoke, his voice was deep and quiet, his eyes probing hers. "When I got to the backyard Tuesday night and Gram said you were in the barn, I thought my heart was going to stop. And then today, when I shouted at you, it was out of fear you would get sick when I desperately want you back on your feet again."

A tear slid down Christine's cheek. "You confuse me."

"I don't mean to," he answered gently.

"It's not you, it's me. Everything confuses me." She began to cry. When she tried to speak, no sound came out and she cried harder.

Luke, unsure of what to say, sat holding her hand and rubbing it gently until she had composed herself. After she had dried her face and looked at Luke, she watched him bow his head. Christine followed suit.

"Dear heavenly Father, thank You for Christine's safety. Thank You for bringing her out of the fire. She was not hurt in the fire, Lord, but she is hurting. Please comfort and heal her. Dry her tears and hold her close. Calm her confusion as only You can do. Help her to trust You, Lord, for her every need, and help me to be here to encourage and care for her. I praise and thank You, God, that You saved Christine and put her in my life. Help us to trust You for our needs and feelings toward each other. In Your Son's holy name I pray. Amen."

Luke was still holding Christine's hand, and after the prayer he reached out and gently touched her cheek. Again their eyes met. "Please don't leave Baxter, Christine. I can't take care of you in Spooner. I can't get to know you if you're so far away. Please don't leave me, Christine, now that I've just found you." The desire to kiss her was almost overpowering, but Luke saw the confusion and fatigue in her eyes.

"I'll go so you can rest. I'll see you tomorrow." Reluctantly he withdrew, knowing that they both needed to be alone with their thoughts and to pray.

39

"Well, Mr. Buelow, please come on in." Maggie answered the front door to find the hotel proprietor on the step.

"I know it's the dinner hour, but I need to see the Doc."

"Of course. I'll get him."

Mark appeared within seconds. "Hello, Al. Good to see you."

"Sorry to get you away from your lunch, but I need to see you."

"Certainly—come on into my office." Mark held open the office door that led off the entryway, and Albert Buelow preceded him inside. When both men were seated Mark said, "Now, what can I do for you?"

"It's not me that needs ya."

"One of your guests?" This was not an unusual occurrence.

"Yeah, we've had a man in number three since the weekend. When we didn't see him around for a few days, Ina thought she should check on him."

"Is he sick?"

"Not exactly. His arm is burned." Mark sat completely still as the weight of this news hit home. Al Buelow watched him, his look one of compassion.

"Is he from around here?"

"I've never seen him before."

"Who else knows about this?"

"Just Ina and myself."

Mark continued to sit very still, his heart hammering in his chest as he asked God for wisdom.

"Al, will you do me a favor?"

"Anything, Doc."

"Go to the sheriff and tell him all you've told me. Also tell him I'm headed over right now to check the man's arm. One more thing, Al—*keep this to yourself.*"

The man nodded solemnly before asking, "How is Miss Bennett?"

"She's doing fine, Al. It was kind of you to ask."

Mark had just seen Al Buelow out when Susanne came into his office. Her smile quickly faded at the look on her husband's face.

"Can you tell me, Mark?"

"There's a man at the hotel with a burned arm." Mark watched the color drain from his wife's face. Sue sat down heavily in the chair that Mark led her to.

"I'm afraid."

"I am too, but we're both being a bit premature. I haven't even examined the man. I'm headed there right now."

"Oh, Mark, please be careful!"

Mark pulled his trembling wife into his arms. "Shhh. You know I'll be careful." He kissed her gently. "Cover me with your prayers." Mark reached for his bag and was gone."

— ❖ —

" 'Bye Silas, thanks for coming."

"Any time. I imagine Luke will be along about suppertime. The buyers today were a little more than we expected. It might not be fair to tell you this, but I could tell his mind was here and not at the ranch."

Christine smiled at him, and he and Grandma Em left the room. If Luke didn't come tonight, she would be tempted to get on a horse and go to him. It was hard to believe how much she wanted to see him.

After much prayer and thought, Christine realized she had been ready to run from the man she loved because anger was clouding her judgment.

In the last 24 hours Christine had done a lot of praying, confessing, and giving over her fears to God. It was time to get to know Luke. They really had shared a very small amount of time together. When he arrived, she planned on telling him that yesterday she had overreacted. She wanted to stay in Baxter in hopes of getting to know him better.

Yet doubts assailed her. Worrying that her approach was too forward, she prayed, "Please help me to know what to say."

Christine reached for her notepaper and scratched out a quick note. Then she moved down in bed to a more comfortable position for a short nap.

"I told ya I didn't want to see no one."

"Well, the doctor's here and he's going to look at that arm." Ina Buelow's hands were planted on her ample hips as she towered over the small, dirty man lying in agony upon one of her beds.

His eyes were clouded with pain, but he tried again. "I tell ya it ain't nothin' but a scratch. Now leave me be."

Mark decided to step in. "I'm Doctor Cameron, and whether or not I look at your arm is entirely up to you. But you *will* answer questions when the sheriff arrives. I can try to alleviate your pain before he comes or you can suffer through the questions."

The small man on the bed sagged with defeat. Or was it relief?

Mark moved forward. The man had a second-degree burn that ran from his left forearm to the back of his hand. He lay quietly, gritting his teeth as Mark examined, cleaned, and wrapped the swollen, oozing skin. By the time Mark finished, the man was bathed in perspiration but hadn't made a sound.

The sheriff had arrived and stood waiting to talk with him. The Buelows left and Mark stood near the door to listen.

Nearly two hours later Mark walked away from the hotel. The man had spent the first half-hour denying there even was a fire. After the sheriff looked around and in the closet found a raggedy overcoat with a badly burned sleeve and a wine bottle with a few tablespoons of kerosene sloshing around in the bottom, the man changed his story.

He insisted that he had been near the barn, but didn't start the fire. He could give no reason for the coat or the wine bottle and nearly came unglued when the sheriff told him the charge for attempted murder was the same in Baxter as it was in Spooner.

The sheriff told Mark when he left that he would be posting a man at the hotel until he could move the burned man to the jail. He never did give his name, but the sheriff planned on holding him until he could wire Spooner.

Mark arrived home to find his brother's horse in front of his house. He was thankful for the saved trip to the ranch.

Silas was on the front-room floor with Emily. They were reading a book together. Much to the delight of his niece, Silas' voice changed with each character.

Mark's cares momentarily evaporated as he listened to the antics of his brother.

The story ended when Emily spotted her dad. She danced around his legs until he swung her up into his arms. Silas folded his long frame into a chair and Mark took the couch.

"Is Luke coming into town tonight?"

"That's a silly question," Silas said with a raised brow.

Mark nodded. "Yes, I suppose it is."

"I just came from Gram's. Christine looks much better," Silas remarked.

"I saw her this morning and she seemed to be coming along. A bit down perhaps, but not physically."

"Luke's arrival will take care of that."

"Do me a favor and ask Luke to stop here when he gets into town."

"Sure, I'll tell him."

"Thanks."

Silas knew better than to ask, but his brother really looked upset about something.

Not long afterward Silas rode toward the ranch, realizing that he could pray even without knowing any details, but his mind kept returning to Luke and Christine. Silas wondered if they had figured out that they were in love. Well, God would take care of it. As Mac liked to say, the Holy Spirit didn't need anyone's help.

The wind had picked up, as did Silas' mount, with both man and beast ready to be home.

40

Luke tied his horse in front of Mark's place and knocked on the door. Mark answered and led Luke wordlessly into his office.

"Al Buelow came over today to tell me a hotel guest was hurt. The man's arm was burned. The sheriff questioned him and he found a burned overcoat and some kerosene hidden in the man's closet. The sheriff plans to hold him until he can get word to and a reply from Spooner."

Luke reeled under the weight of the news. He leaned against the wall, feeling as if the pins had been knocked out from under him.

Mark let Luke catch his breath before saying, "I don't know how to tell Christine without upsetting her."

"We won't tell her," Luke replied after some moments.

"What?"

"I said we won't tell her," Luke repeated calmly.

"Luke, that's not fair. She has a right to know."

"It will only frighten her. Anyway, the man is in custody. It's over now."

"Luke, it's not over. Christine is not dead and I'm sure whoever wants her that way will not give up so easily." Mark knew the words were harsh, but he could see the need to be blunt.

"I'll be here to take care of her."

"Luke, be reasonable. Even if you two were married, you wouldn't be with her all the time. She needs to know about this so she can be on her guard and less vulnerable. She's not a little girl, Luke. We can't protect and treat her like one."

Mark continued on in his argument, but Luke was adamant. Mark even considered going to Christine himself, but put the idea away when he saw how single-minded Luke was to keep the information from her. He watched his brother leave, a heavy feeling in Mark's heart.

The ride to his grandmother's house was short, but in that span Luke was even more determined to keep the recent developments from Christine and to proceed as he hoped. By the time Luke arrived and found his grandmother in the kitchen, he had nearly succeeded in pushing the barn fire from his mind.

"I found this on Christine's bedside table when I checked on her." Grandma Em handed him the note.

> Grandma Em, please wake me if Luke comes.
> Don't let him leave.

"Is she awake yet?" Luke asked, still holding the note.

"I don't think so. It's pretty quiet up there."

Luke began to pace. "Was she upset? Did she tell you why she had to see me?"

Grandma Em opened her mouth to answer when they both heard a sneeze. Luke gave his grandmother a small smile and walked with a determined stride up to Christine's room.

The room was chilly and Christine was settled back against the pillow, the quilts tucked in tight around her. She heard someone on the stairs and watched as Luke came in. He was without a doubt a man with a purpose.

Not a word was spoken as Luke moved the desk chair to the head of the bed and leaned close to Christine, much like yesterday.

"I've done a lot of thinking since yesterday, Christine. I was insensitive to your needs and I'm sorry." Luke leaned a bit closer, his voice almost urgent. "I realized after I left yesterday that we've had almost no time together." Luke hesitated, knowing it was too soon to tell her he loved her.

"I care deeply for you, Christine. And I want you to stay in Baxter. Stay and give us time to get to know each other. I can't believe how little I know about you. We've both lost our parents and I think we have a lot to share. Please stay, Christine; give us a chance."

A tiny bubble of laughter, in contrast with the tears sparkling in her eyes, sounded from Christine's throat. "I had the same speech planned for you."

"You mean about staying in Baxter and getting to know each other?"

Christine gave him a happy nod. Luke's laughter sounded through the upstairs and Christine joined him. Their relief was more precious because they had both asked for God's guidance.

Christine touched Luke's arm. "I need to say something else. I'm sorry about the way I acted yesterday. I've never been a good patient."

"Oh, really! I hadn't noticed." Christine bit her lip in an effort to keep from smiling, knowing that if she did he would only be encouraged to tease her more.

When Christine asked Luke to give her a few minutes alone he left the room, shutting the door behind him, and waited in the hall. Supper aromas were drifting up the stairs, and he decided that he and Grandma Em should bring their plates up and eat with Christine.

"All set!" Luke turned in surprise at Christine's voice as she came out into the hall, dressed and wrapped in a quilt. She smiled at him as she moved toward the stairs. "I'm starved." Christine spoke again and was partway down the stairs before she realized that Luke had not followed.

Christine stopped and spoke without turning, "I'm fine, Luke. My throat doesn't hurt, and if I have to stay in that bed another minute I'll go out of my mind." Christine was relieved when she heard Luke move onto the steps behind her.

His presence was so comforting. She had to stop herself

from leaning into him as he reached her on the stairs and put his hand on her back to guide her to the parlor.

"I rather thought I'd see you down here tonight, Christine." Grandma Em's eyes twinkled with mischief as she kissed Christine's cheek. "Your room is lovely, but 24 hours a day gets to be a bit much."

Grandma Em went back to the stove. Christine put her quilt on a chair, intending to follow. She had only stepped twice before she felt the quilt drop back onto her shoulders and Luke's hands guide her to a seat.

"I need to help," she protested after he had sat her down.

"I'll help her."

"Luke, I can't just sit here."

"Yes, you can." Christine heard the words correctly but knew that his look and tone were really saying, "You had better."

Luke, who was bent over Christine to talk quietly into her upturned face, saw the exact moment she gave in. His knuckles brushed feather-lightly down her cheek before he moved to aid his grandmother.

Christine's earlier statement of being starved had not been far from the truth. She filled her plate twice and had two pieces of pie.

"That was delicious." Christine sat back with a sigh.

"Did you think I had forgotten how to cook?" Grandma Em asked with feigned indignation.

"No!" Christine laughed.

"Well, the truth is, you do have me pretty spoiled."

"What I'd really like to do is spoil you some more by doing the dishes. But," Christine continued quickly as Luke began to protest, "your grandson has other ideas. So I'm headed to the parlor so I won't have to watch you work."

After Christine left, Luke began to gather the plates, but Grandma Em waved him away. "I can get them, Luke. Go sit with Christine."

Luke, much to his grandmother's amusement, didn't

even hesitate. He found Christine curled up on the couch and he joined her.

"Are you warm enough?"

Christine nodded in contentment, willing to just sit with Luke in comfortable silence. She was feeling tired and Luke also was content to just be near her.

As the silence between them continued, Luke grew pensive. His thoughts were turning bleak before he realized that Christine had leaned forward and was looking into his face.

"Did I cause that scowl?"

"No." Luke reined his thoughts in and smiled into Christine's eyes. Christine realized she was leaning rather close. Hastily she sat back and began to nervously pleat the quilt in her lap. "Tell me about your ranch." Christine spoke, wishing she couldn't feel his eyes on her.

"No."

"What!" Christine felt a bit taken aback at his abrupt answer.

"I said no, because I want you to come and see the ranch. Next Friday."

"I'll have to check with Grandma Em." Christine smiled with relief. "But I'd love to."

The next few hours flew by. Grandma Em finished the dishes and the three sat in the parlor. Talk moved rapidly from one subject to the next.

When Luke was ready to leave, Christine walked him to the door. With his coat and hat on, he leaned against the door and took Christine's hand.

"I won't see you tomorrow. But," he said with mock sternness, "I expect to hear that you rested and took it easy when I get here Sunday." He pointed a finger at her. "Do I make myself clear, Christine Bennett?"

"Yes, sir!" Christine spoke with exaggerated sweetness.

Luke only groaned and rolled his eyes, knowing she would do exactly as she pleased. This groan brought a smile to Christine's face.

Suddenly Christine knew she was about to be kissed. She couldn't stop the tensing in her body, the clenching of her hands at her side.

Luke didn't miss her stance. She looked like a frightened animal about to bolt. Slow down, Luke, he told himself—don't rush her.

Careful not to move toward her in any way, Luke let go of her hand and reached for the door handle. "Good night, Christine. I'll see you Sunday."

"Good night." Christine stood for a long time after the door shut, the cold air no longer swirling around her legs. "If I didn't want Luke to kiss me, why am I so disappointed that he didn't?"

Long after Christine bid Grandma Em good night and took herself off to bed, the question plagued her.

41

"Come in," Christine called to the knock on her bedroom door, assuming it was Grandma Em this early on a Sunday morning. "Oh, Mark! It's you!" Christine sent up a quick prayer of thanks that she was dressed.

Mark came into the room and saw that his brother's suspicions had been right: Christine was ready for church. He also wondered absently how Christine was able to tell him and Luke apart, no matter what they were wearing.

"I'm on a mission for my brother," Mark said.

Christine laughed, feeling quite certain she knew what that mission was. "Why don't you tell me about it over a cup of coffee."

"Lead the way," Mark said as he gestured gallantly toward the door.

"So," Christine said after she had put the coffee on, "what's up? I assume when you say 'brother,' you are referring to Luke?"

"Correct. Luke wants me to make sure you are well enough to be out today, and if not, to make you go back to bed."

Again Christine laughed. "What would you like to know? My throat feels fine. My eyes and nose no longer burn. My leg is still tender and I think the skin is going to peel. I must admit I tire easily, but I just rest when I feel the need. Other than the fact that the animals are not here to feed, it's almost as if the fire never happened." Christine shrugged and moved to get the coffee.

Mark watched as she poured two cups. "Yes," he thought, "she's ready to be out again." Unbidden, another thought followed: "It's easier to keep her safe if she stays in."

"Mark, if that look on your face means you're about to tell me to go back to bed, then I best warn you, you'll have a fight on your hands."

Mark looked up to see that Christine had put the coffeepot back on the stove. Her hands were planted on her hips, her chin was thrust out, and she was ready for a battle.

Mark could not keep the smile from his face. "Luke, my dear brother," he thought to himself, "you have met your match."

Christine's battle stance turned to confusion upon seeing that smile. She watched as Mark drained his coffeecup, amazed that he could drink it so hot. Standing, he said, "I'll see you in church, Christine," and then he was out the door.

"And men think women are hard to explain," Christine said to a supposedly empty room some minutes later.

"There's no hope for you, Christine, if you're talking to yourself at 19. What are you going to be doing at my age?"

The women shared a good laugh and Christine explained Mark's visit, none of which was news to Grandma Em. She didn't miss much of the goings-on in her family.

The women took some time to pray and share a verse before starting breakfast. Christine had begun to memorize Scripture. Reading Psalm 121 for the first time the night before, she had determined to put all eight verses to memory.

Luke and Silas came in to find Grandma Em setting the table for breakfast and Christine stirring the cooked cereal with one hand and holding a Bible in the other, completely engrossed. Luke asked his grandmother what Christine was doing, and he was not surprised at the answer, for he was learning that Christine did most things with a fierce sense of purpose.

Silas had stepped to the stove to pour a cup of coffee. "Memorizing is hard work."

"I think so, and it gets harder as you get older," Silas replied. "I can't believe how fast the kids can learn those verses. Of course Julia is an exception—she can memorize today as well as she could when we were kids. She used to beat the pants off us boys. Maybe it was the Lord's way of making her extra-special. Being raised with three older brothers who were always a little faster and stronger has a way of discouraging a girl. Even when she stopped competing with us and began to grow up, we teased her for putting her hair up or wearing ribbons. Not until she turned 15 and fell so hard for Mac did we have any compassion."

Luke came out to the kitchen, and he and Christine exchanged a smile before Christine turned back to Silas.

"Were you really compassionate toward her?"

"I don't think we ever said anything to her, but I sure remember the day after she told Mac she couldn't see him again. All the sparkle went out of her."

Luke joined the conversation at this point. "She did her work and never complained, but when we teased her, there was no reaction. It went on like that for nearly a month before our father blew his stack."

"That was a bad night," Silas went on. "It was at the supper table. He really raked her over the coals. Told her to stop moping around and get back into the family or he'd find so much work for her to do that she'd have no time to pout."

"Julia was already doing the work of a grown woman and had been since her mother died." Grandma Em had come in and talked as she cracked eggs into a pan. "We all make mistakes, and I'm afraid that was one of Joseph Jr.'s worst."

Breakfast preparation was finished in silence and the four sat around the table. Prayer was said and they began to eat before Luke continued the story.

"Julia came around after that. She would laugh and talk with us when we were around. But she also lost weight and spent more time alone than she ever had in her life. It was as if she decided on her own to take Dad's word and to work to forget Mac."

Silas shook his head and took off where Luke had finished. "She never stopped working. Dad began to see that he'd been too harsh with her. Then she got sick. She was down to skin and bones and collapsed one day in the kitchen. Paul found her and came for us in the stable. She burned up with fever for three days. It was during this time that we found out just how painful it had been to tell Mac she couldn't see him.

"She kept saying, 'I'm sorry, Mac, I had to obey my father. I don't think I'm too good for you. I love you, but I have to obey my father. Please, God, please save Mac and help him understand.' It never came out at one time, but she would cry and talk. Paul never left her side, and he heard most of it.

"Paul became Julia's champion. He told all of us, including our father, that we'd been unfair and that we owed her an apology and some help with the work around the house.

"He cried, didn't he, Luke? And he told the family that if things didn't change, he and Julia were going to move into town to Grandpa's. He was so upset after his speech that he wouldn't even speak with us."

It was time to do the dishes or they would be late for church. As they worked, Luke finished the story.

"It took Julia some time to get back on her feet. While she convalesced, Silas did most of the housework and we helped. He became a very good cook, by the way. Anyhow, after Julia was up and about, we all apologized to her and promised to help her with her work. We also began to pray daily as a family for Mac's salvation. Having us behind her turned Julia around. She became her old self, and it wasn't long afterward that Mac came to church. He began to eat Sunday dinner with us, and one day Paul led him to the Lord. Now, eight years of marriage later and two little boys down the road, it's just like Silas said—she can still memorize with the best of them."

Christine was amazed at Julia's story. Julia had said that things had been hard, but she had never once hinted at the real pain she had experienced. These thoughts stayed with Christine until the four of them bundled into the wagon and headed for church.

The proximity of Luke on the rear seat with her drove away all thought of Julia as Christine reached between them to steady herself on the seat. Luke took her hand, holding it all the way to church.

He released her hand only after the wagon had stopped in the churchyard.

They had arrived in time for the service, and in the few minutes before it started Luke asked Christine about her memorizing.

"Gram tells me you're working on Psalm 121. How is it going?"

"Well, I just started last night. I read it and read it, then close my Bible and can't remember a thing."

Luke laughed softly and Christine studied his face. He looked so tan against the crisp whiteness of his dress shirt. His hair was a little mussed from the wagon ride and a few stray locks fell on his forehead. His teeth and smile were beautiful. And those eyes! Sapphire! Christine looked away—how would she ever concentrate on the sermon?

Mrs. Nolan had started the piano prelude, and Luke quickly leaned over to Christine. "I worked in Psalm 121 when I was a kid. I could use a refresher course. Why don't we work on it together?"

Christine's look was uncertain and Luke misinterpreted it. "If you'd rather not..."

"No, it's not that..." Christine was not allowed to explain because Pastor Nolan had stepped to the front.

The sermon was on fear—specifically, the giving over of fear to God. Christine and Grandma Em had talked on this subject several times, and Pastor Nolan confirmed much of what she had said. "When we start to feel that some fear will overwhelm us, we should immediately pray and keep praying until we've given that fear to God and can rest in Him," Grandma Em had said.

Luke seemed restless, Christine thought, but then maybe she had imagined it.

Pastor Nolan ended his sermon by suggesting some good verses to refer to when fears assailed. Joshua 1:9: "Have not I commanded thee? Be strong and of good courage; be not afraid, neither be thou dismayed, for the Lord thy God is with thee wherever thou goest." Psalm 27:1: "The Lord is my light and my salvation; whom shall I fear? The Lord is the strength of my life; of whom shall I be afraid?" Hebrews 13:6: "We may boldly say, 'The Lord is my helper, and I will not fear what man shall do unto me.'" Isaiah 41:10: "Fear thou not, for I am with thee; be not dismayed, for I am thy God. I will strengthen thee; yea, I will help thee; yea, I will uphold thee with the right hand of my righteousness."

The service closed with the congregation standing and reading the 23rd Psalm. Christine noticed that Luke recited it from memory. Christine was discouraged as she left church. There was so much to learn. With this on her mind, Christine failed to notice Luke's rather quiet demeanor on the way home.

42

Luke thought much about the sermon on the wagon ride home. He felt very convicted about not giving his fears to God. It was fear, plain and simple, that kept Luke from telling Christine about the burned man at the hotel—fear that she would panic and go back to Spooner, and he would lose her forever.

These thoughts rode him hard, even as they arrived back at Grandma Em's and went in for Sunday dinner.

"There's my girl." Susanne spoke tenderly to her infant daughter as she transferred her to Christine's arms. "Fed and dry, Christine, you're getting Eliza at her best."

Christine laughed softly. "I never would have believed how much fun it could be to be chased out of the kitchen. I put up a fight, but Julia was adamant. I'll have to thank her."

The two women were in Grandma Em's room. Sue buttoned her blouse as Christine gently rocked the baby. The usually quiet Sue surprised Christine when she broke the silence with a question.

"Should we be asking God to give you a baby, Christine?"

Christine's look was so startled that Sue laughed.

"Don't you think I should start with a husband?" Christine finally asked.

"Do you have anyone in mind?" When Christine didn't answer the question, Sue went on. "If you don't, I do."

"I rather thought you might. Does he happen to be the spitting image of your husband?"

Susanne smiled, not at all sheepish about being so transparent. "It is a nice face to wake up to every day." When Christine blushed, Sue went on softly. "If Luke lets you get away, Christine, I may never speak to him again."

A few minutes later there was a soft knock on the door and Mark entered. He joined his wife on the edge of the bed and smiled at the sight of Elizabeth on Christine's shoulder.

"I was just asking Christine if we needed to ask God for a baby for her."

"Don't you think she should start with a husband?"

"Who should start with a husband?" Christine could hardly believe her ears. How could a man of his size move so quietly?

Luke stood patiently awaiting an answer. When none came, he approached the rocking chair and knelt down next to Christine and Elizabeth. Christine watched him look at the baby before turning his attention to her. "She's too fair to be...yours." Luke stopped just short of saying ours, and Christine didn't miss the pause.

"I would take her anyhow." Christine spoke quickly, hoping to direct Luke's attention back to his niece, but to no avail—his eyes were still searching her face.

Christine was glad of Sue's interruption just then. She took the baby and put her in the basket by the bed. All four adults quietly left the room. Mark and Sue led the way down the stairs. When it was Christine's turn to follow, she held back, causing Luke to stop behind her.

Turning, she asked, "Luke, is anything bothering you?"

"Tell her, Luke," an inner voice prompted. "Tell her about the man at the hotel." But when he spoke, it was only "No."

Christine smiled at him, thinking again that she had imagined his restlessness at church.

The day sped by with good food and fellowship. Christine was moved away from the kitchen every time she headed that way, even for the most innocent of reasons.

By the time Luke said goodbye, with the time drawing near for the horses to be fed, Christine had completely forgotten that she had thought something was wrong. Luke had been happy and charming all afternoon. They had worked together on Christine's memory verses. Laughing away her earlier hesitation that stemmed from a fear of not being able to memorize all eight verses, Luke said they would take as much time to memorize together as they needed.

Twice he had held her hand, once at the dinner table and again after she had read Emily a story. Christine climbed into bed that night with a glow about her as she remembered the way Emily had fallen asleep in her lap and the way Luke had reached for her hand and held it between them. She marveled again at the way he made her feel little and protected with the mere act of placing her hand in his.

With these happy thoughts Christine fell asleep, praising God for love, happiness, and Luke Cameron.

43

"It snowed! It snowed!"

Mac squinted up at the little boy sitting in the middle of his chest. Beside him he heard Julia's breath leave her in a rush as Charles landed on her stomach, enroute to joining his brother.

"It snowed, Papa," Charles added, in case his father had missed Calvin's words.

"And you two are going to see that I can't enjoy it by crushing my chest!" The boys grinned indulgently at their father. Both were quite sure that *nothing* could crush John MacDonald's chest.

"We prayed and God sent the snow, didn't we, Cal? We prayed every night in our beds."

"Charlie's right. We prayed and asked God to send it for Thanksgiving. We asked for Christine."

Mac had pulled Julia close, and with her head pillowed on Mac's shoulder she asked, "Why for Christine?"

"Because that day she came out to swing with us, she told me and Cal that she'd never been in a snowball fight."

Mac cleared his throat. "That was very kind of you boys to think of Christine. I'm proud of you."

"Don't cry, Mama! The snow is here. It's okay now." Charles' concerned look and caring words just caused Julia to cry harder. Mac reached past her for the handkerchief she usually kept under her pillow.

After handing it to Julia, Mac again spoke to the boys. "Your mother's tears are because she is just as proud of you as I am, that you prayed and thought of Christine's happiness."

"Is Christine going to marry Uncle Luke?"

"Why do you ask, Charles?" Julia asked as she dried her face.

"They were holding hands on Sunday and Uncle Luke smiles a lot."

"Yeah," Charles joined in. "He still plays and talks with us, but his eyes are always watching Christine."

"Well, I think that Luke and Christine care for each other, but marriage is a big step, and until they decide what they want and share it with us—" Mac paused here to make sure he had both boys' attention—"we are not going to ask them or bring the subject up. Understood?" Both boys nodded solemnly. "Okay, go get bundled up. We've got some shoveling to do."

The boy's shouts and laughter echoed back to Mac and Julia's ears as they ran for their room.

"What's the frown for?"

"Well, you just told the boys we're not going to ask Luke and Christine what's going on, and I was hoping you would talk to Luke and find out how he feels."

"Julia, my sweet, that is none of our business." His voice was patient.

"I know! That is precisely why I was trying to figure a way to find out." She stated this so matter-of-factly that Mac burst into gales of laughter. Julia hit him with a pillow, but to no avail. He was still chuckling when he was dressed and ready to leave the room.

He bent over Julia, who was buried beneath the covers in bed, his face close to hers.

"Do you know what I'm thankful for?"

Julia smiled, sure she would hear a loving endearment.

"I'm thankful that being married to Julia means never being bored." Mac kissed the tip of her nose and scooted toward the door. He slipped out an instant before another pillow sailed through the air.

— ⚜ —

"Go ahead, Luke, I don't mind staying."

"Don't be ridiculous. I'm not leaving you here."

"You haven't seen Christine since Sunday. Go, Luke! It doesn't take both of us to check on this colt."

"Forget it, Silas! We're in this together and I won't hear another word about it."

Silas turned away. When Luke made up his mind, there was no swaying him.

The men had come out that morning to find a mare had foaled unexpectedly. The colt seemed to be all right, but it was small, and for the sake of both horses it was best to be sure there was no problem.

So Luke stubbornly stood at the stall of the first-time mother and newborn colt, thankful for its safe arrival but wishing he could be with Christine.

— ✛ —

"I hate having Paul gone on the holidays. You wouldn't think with the mob we'll have here that I could miss anyone, but I do." Grandma Em's voice was wistful.

"Who is Paul the most like?"

"Oh, he's such a combination, yet he's his own person. He's a wonderful listener like Si and a gentle presence like Mark. But he can also be very commanding and behave like Luke. And like Julia, there's also that side of him that flaunts convention."

"He sounds too good to be true."

"No, no. He's far from perfect! He struggles with doubts and fears, and they sometimes get the best of him."

"You never did say what you were the most thankful for in Paul's life."

Grandma Em stopped her peeling and looked thoughtful. "I guess I'm most thankful he went to seminary school. It was no easy decision, I can tell you. He was so unhappy at the ranch. He'd been raised with those horses but he wasn't satisfied to stay on, as Luke and Silas were. He considered going into medicine. He even went out with Mark a few times, but it just wasn't for him. His letters home are filled with the joy of the Lord. So I guess I'm thankful he's where he's supposed to be and happy about it."

The women went on with their dinner preparation. The turkey was cooking and the potatoes were peeled. Christine was working on pumpkin and mincemeat pies. Both Julia and Susanne were bringing dishes so that everything would not be left to Grandma Em and Christine.

"You never asked me what I'm thankful for today."

Grandma Em looked surprised. "You're right, I didn't. Will you tell me now?" she asked kindly.

"I'm thankful for you," Christine answered with her head down, her voice quiet and thick with tears as she rolled out the pie dough. She stopped when she felt Grandma Em at her side. The women hugged and cried silently for a time.

"Do you remember how awful our first meeting was?"

"Yes, I was scared to death of you."

"I said that awful thing about you stealing."

Both women found this all highly amusing. So when the MacDonald family entered a few minutes later, it was to find Christine and Grandma Em with the giggles, their eyes still wet with tears.

Mac hugged both women and then stood regarding them in turn. "There must be something in the air. Julia has been crying today too."

"Ours were tears of joy," Christine told him.

"Hers were too," he smiled back at her.

"Well, look at you two!" Grandma Em spoke to the little boys standing around Mac's legs. "You look like you're ready to brave the snow."

We're here for Christine," Calvin announced.

That's right, we're going to show her how to have a snowball fight."

Christine laughed with delight and knelt down to pull both heavily garbed boys into her arms. They both became suddenly shy, and Christine said, "I'll go get ready."

— ⚜ —

"Not very good, am I?"

Trying to be tactful, Calvin hesitated, but Charles spoke right out.

"You're a terrible thrower, Christine! You haven't hit a thing you've aimed at!"

"Well, she throws it pretty far, though—just not in the right direction." Calvin spoke now in an effort to soften Charles' words.

Christine bit her lip to keep from laughing out loud. The boys were so serious. Charles had generously taken her onto his team against Calvin, but Calvin was killing them. He never missed. Charles was a fair shot, but Christine was awful. She tried to be optimistic.

"Well, it's my first time. Let's try it again." The boys were agreeable and they spent some time building up their arsenal.

"Okay, I think we're ready." With that the war was on in earnest. What Christine lost in throwing she made up for in ducking Calvin's barrage. At one point he took her by surprise and hit her right on the side of the head. She let out a false bellow of rage that had both boys in stitches before winding up like a pro and letting a snowball fly. As usual, her aim was quite poor at best, but she did hit someone, causing all three snowball throwers to become deathly quiet and watch as Luke wiped the snow from his face. Knowing beyond a shadow of doubt that Christine's throw was a mistake, Luke couldn't pass up the opportunity to tackle her into the snow.

Her cheeks were cherry red with the cold and her eyes were bright with suppressed laughter. Her hat was tilted a bit and had snow on one side. Luke couldn't think when she had ever looked more beautiful.

He spoke slowly as he approached. "So this is the way I'm treated when I don't see you for three days!"

"It was an accident, I'm sorry," Christine said on a bubble of laughter.

"Oh, you sound very sorry!" Luke fought his own mirth.

This made Christine laugh harder, and she began to back away. "What are you going to do to me?"

Luke smiled at this question and Christine, a little afraid of that smile, turned and ran. She had rounded the far end of the house and thought freedom was in sight when her legs went out from under her.

Christine rolled onto her back and put both hands up to wipe the snow from her face. When she felt Luke's hands join her own, she looked up to see him kneeling beside her.

It was on the tip of her tongue to tell him what a rascal he was for knocking her in the snow, but he was leaning over her now, his eyes locked with hers, his lips descending.

"Christine," he breathed, his lips nearly touching hers.

"We'll save you, Christine!" The spell was broken. Calvin's gallant cry reached them.

Before the boys could round the corner of the house, Luke helped Christine to her feet. He pulled her into his arms and held her close under the guise of dusting the snow off her back. The boys bounced on to the scene just as he released her.

Even as the boys danced around their legs, Luke and Christine's eyes locked once again. "I'm sorry," Christine said, the words for his ears alone. Luke took her hand and squeezed it gently. "Later," she heard him say. The look in his eyes told Christine it was a promise he would keep.

44

The dishes were done and Susanne had just fed Elizabeth and put her down for a nap. Grandma Em called everyone into the front room. Christine was surprised as Silas sat down at the piano and played a few hymns. Everyone sang and then Grandma Em asked the children to share what they were thankful for.

Emily was thankful for a new sister and that she only cried some of the time. Charles was thankful for the snow and for turkey dinner. Calvin made Christine cry when he expressed thanks for snow and that Christine had played with them.

Luke and Christine had no time alone together, but Christine was thrilled at the way he stayed by her side throughout the day.

The day was a long and happy one. It was late before Luke and Silas left. If Christine hadn't known she would see him the next morning, she would have begged him to stay.

After Christine climbed into bed, she kept the lamp turned up and reached for her Bible. Holding it unopened, she began to pray.

Christine thanked God for the wonderful family to whom He had brought her. She knew in her heart that God had led her right to them. Tears slid down her cheeks as she thought of her grandfather, wishing with all her heart he could have met Luke and his family. She knew they would have liked one another.

Christine fell asleep hoping that at some time her grandfather had made that step of faith. She asked God to help her keep from dwelling on the subject and to go on from where she was, in obedience to His will and not to fret about things she couldn't change.

Visions of Luke and the ranch floated through her mind. Tomorrow! Tomorrow she would see him again.

45

"Ready to go?" Luke asked the women who stood before him.

"We've been ready to go since—"

"Yes, we're ready!" Christine interrupted Grandma Em loudly and sent her a pleading look. But it was too late.

"Up early, Christine?" Luke asked innocently.

"What makes you think that?" Christine threw over her shoulder as she moved through the snow toward the cutter.

The three of them on the seat was a tight fit, but it was nice for warmth. Christine was thankful that Luke had dropped the subject of when she awoke. She was not at all willing for him to know she had awakened very early and had paced until it was time to go.

Luke had his own reasons for not rekindling the subject. He too had risen some two hours earlier than usual and had made coffee and tried to read but ended up pacing just like Christine.

Baxter was a world of white, much to Christine's enjoyment. The trees and housetops were powdered and glistening in the morning sun.

Grandma Em was snuggled for warmth between Luke and Christine, and Christine was able to lean over the side and watch the sleigh runners race along the snow-covered ground. Her attention was brought back to the road when the horse snorted loudly and picked up his pace; home was in sight.

Christine's first close-up look of the Cameron ranch house was a sight she would never forget.

The rectangular snow-covered roof sported two chimneys, both billowing smoke. The front door, off-center and to the left, was preceded by a wide, multipillared porch.

Luke pulled up in front of the porch and surprised Christine when he took her by the waist and swung her all the way onto it. Grandma Em was shortly beside her and Silas was out to bustle them into the house.

Grandma Em went directly to the fire burning in the stove. Christine stood admiring the immense room. It was a combination front room, kitchen, and dining room. She took in the beautiful oak furnishings, from the piano to the kitchen table.

Everything was orderly, though not without its bachelor touches: a stack of papers spread across a table by the sofa, a pair of boots standing in the corner with socks dangling from the top. The atmosphere was welcoming and this made Christine smile.

"I hope that smile means you approve." Luke was standing beside her, intently watching her face.

"I think your home is wonderful!" Christine replied in all seriousness.

"Why don't I show you the stables before you take off your coat?"

Christine readily agreed. She and Luke walked down to the stables, Luke leading the horse and cutter.

Christine stepped in when Luke threw the door open wide to admit the sleigh. She breathed deeply of the familiar aromas of hay, horses, and leather. Rows of windows allowed the November sun to stream in and take some of the chill from the air.

Christine walked along the stalls, admiring the beautiful coats and healthy looks of the Camerons' quarter horses.

Luke went to park the cutter and rub down his horse. Christine had continued her tour until she came to a stall that housed the most magnificent black stallion she had ever seen.

She stepped close to speak softly with him. "Hello there, fella. What's your name? Oh, you are a beauty! You remind me of Raven."

"Who's Raven?" Luke spoke from his place at Christine's side. She was growing accustomed to the way he could move so silently.

"Raven is my horse in Spooner."

"Is she as black as her name?"

"Yes. I helped our coachman with her birth, and when he saw her he said, 'She's as black as a raven's wing.' The next day my grandfather reminded me she had been born after midnight and on my sixteenth birthday. He gave her to me and I named her Raven." Christine stopped abruptly, feeling as though she were babbling, but Luke was fascinated.

"When is your birthday?"

"Next month."

"What day?"

"The 24th."

"The 24th! You're a Christmas Eve baby! Christine for Christmas Eve." Luke sounded delighted, but Christine was a bit embarrassed. She wished sometimes that he wouldn't watch her so intently. It was most unsettling.

"Does anyone call you Christie?" In his mind she had been Christie for some time.

"My grandfather used to. And his housekeeper, Mrs. Hall, still does."

Christine moved down the stalls then to escape those blue eyes that were able to frustrate and confuse her so.

Luke followed along, giving a short history of any horse that Christine showed an interest in. She was delighted with several foals, and Luke returned to the subject of Raven's birth. They discussed it further and he was impressed with how knowledgeable she was.

They were about halfway through when Luke asked, "Are you warm enough?"

"Oh, yes, this coat is very warm."

"I don't think I've ever told you, but it looks wonderful on you."

Christine hated herself for it, but she was embarrassed by the compliment, so she changed the subject.

"Luke, I've been meaning to ask you. How did you get to Grandma Em's ahead of me on the day my coat arrived?"

"It's no great trick, Christine, I assure you," Luke answered with a smile. "You were so angry that you didn't even see me ride directly past you."

"Oh," was all Christine could think to say before moving along and looking into the next stall. She stood for a few minutes watching the very pregnant mare within before turning to ask Luke about the animal.

To Christine's surprise Luke had stepped directly behind her, so that when she turned she found herself face-to-face with him as he bent slightly over her.

Christine couldn't move, so trapped was she by the love she saw written in his eyes.

"Christie," Luke spoke as his hands came up to frame her face, his lips brushing her forehead and then her cheek.

"I'm in love with you, Christie." The words came out in a breathless whisper just before his lips met hers.

Christine's hands came up to cling to Luke's arms in an attempt to steady herself as Luke tenderly kissed her. It was brief and sweet, and when Luke raised his head, Christine felt her hat being tugged off. Luke touched the thick tresses that fell from beneath the hat and marveled at the softness.

"I've wanted to touch your hair for so long, to see if it's as soft as it looks."

"I've been tempted to cut it many times." Christine's voice was little more than a whisper.

"If you ever cut it, I'll paddle you." Luke spoke before once again lowering his head. It was the most natural thing in the world when Luke broke the kiss for Christine to share what was in her heart.

"I love you, Luke."

"Oh, Christie, Christie, I had begun to think I would never hear you say those words. I could see it in your eyes, but I was afraid you would be too shy to say them. When, Christie, when did you first know?"

"The Sunday morning I spilled coffee on your pants and you tried so hard not to show your irritation. When was it for you?

"Well, I must admit I was attracted to you immediately, but with you not knowing Christ, I took special care to keep the attraction in check. For me it was the night of the fire. I knew when I carried you away from the barn that I wouldn't be feeling the way I did about almost losing you if I didn't love you."

Christine beamed as she heard the words again.

"Do you know how close you come to getting kissed every time I see that smile?"

"I think so. It makes me a little bit afraid of you."

"Really, I hadn't noticed!"

Christine shook her head at him. "Calvin is right. You *are* a terrible tease!" They had begun to walk toward the door, but Luke stopped abruptly.

"Christie, did I make you cry the Sunday I teased you at Mark and Sue's?"

"No, it wasn't your teasing." She tried to keep walking, but Luke pulled her to him.

"Please tell me, Christie."

Christine hesitated and then sighed. "I had finally begun to admit to myself that I was in love with you, and when I saw you and Caroline on the couch together with Elizabeth, I thought it was hopeless." Christine's words came out with heavy reluctance, and she didn't look at Luke. "Caroline is so dainty and fair. I felt as big as Mac and as dark as a thundercloud."

"Christie!" Two fingers beneath Christine's chin tipped her head back until she was looking Luke in the eye. The tenderness she saw there, combined with the loving way he said her nickname, had a way of breaking down all her defenses.

"Caroline Chambers is a sweet, rather spoiled girl, and I do mean girl. I am in love with a woman—a tall, beautiful woman whose green eyes and chestnut-colored hair drive me to distraction."

He pulled her into his arms then and once again kissed her thoroughly.

Christine couldn't remember the walk back to the house. She was once again on the front porch with Luke, and he was telling her he loved her. He didn't kiss her this time, but held her close before opening the door to the warmth within.

46

"I think it's snowing too hard for Grandma Em and Christine to go home."

Silas looked at the miniscule flakes barely falling out of the sky. The men were walking to the stables, and Silas' laughter echoed in the cold air.

"Are you afraid Christine is going to get away from you if you let her out of your sight?"

Luke was disgusted at Silas' lack of sympathy. "You just wait, little brother"—a ridiculous statement, since Silas was only an inch shorter than the twins and a year younger. "When you fall in love, it will be *my* turn to give *you* a hard time."

Silas was undaunted. "Oh, so you've finally figured out you're in love?"

"What's that supposed to mean?"

"Well, I've known for some time."

"Is that a fact?"

"Sure, a blind man could see it. Christine blushed to the roots of her hair every time you got within ten feet of her, and you spent most of your time trying *not* to look at her."

Luke stopped dead in his tracks, so accurate was the description of his and Christine's relationship a few weeks back. Silas just thumped him on the chest and walked into the barn, still laughing. He was most pleased with himself.

— ✧ —

"Do you think it will snow too hard for us to get home?" Christine asked Grandma Em, trying not to sound too excited.

"I take it you'd rather like spending time with Luke?" Grandma Em asked kindly, wanting very much to laugh.

199

"Does it bother you that I'm... interested in Luke? Would you rather we didn't care for each other?" Grandma Em *did* laugh then. Christine was such a delightful combination of confidence and insecurity. Luke would certainly never be bored with this woman.

"Christine, I would love nothing more than to see you and Luke in love, married and filling these bedrooms with babies."

Christine was surprised speechless. Marriage? She had not thought that far. It caused an incredible flood of apprehension and worries to flow through her head. Was Luke thinking of marriage? What about all the unsolved trouble in Spooner? Maybe Luke didn't really know everything, and if he did, would he still want to marry her?

"Christine, your face tells me I just opened a Pandora's box," Grandma Em said as she poured two cups of coffee.

Not until after Christine was seated and sipping her coffee did Grandma Em speak again.

"It was not my intention to interfere, Christine. What you and Luke do is between the two of you. I'm sorry if I upset you."

"You haven't upset me—it's just that I hadn't thought as far ahead as marriage. It's not that the idea is unappealing; it's just new to me and takes a bit of getting used to."

Grandma Em reached for and patted Christine's hand. "Believe it or not, Christine, I know what you're feeling. Joseph asked me to marry him four weeks after we met. He scared me to death."

"What did you do?"

"I ran."

"You ran away?" Christine was incredulous. Emily Cameron was not a woman who ran from anything.

Grandma Em nodded slowly. "I told my mother I wanted to go visit my aunt, who lived about 30 miles away. I was there for nearly two weeks before Joseph showed up. He was furious.

"The three of us—Joseph, my aunt, and I—sat in the parlor and talked for a bit. Aunt Eleanor was thrilled that a young man had come to see me. She was sure that at 20 years of age I was destined to be an old maid. So when Joseph asked if we could go for a stroll she was delighted, and I had no time to protest as he nearly dragged me out of the house. I remember we walked and walked. He was so angry that he didn't even speak. When we finally did stop, he turned to me with such pain-filled eyes that it nearly broke my heart.

"We talked for hours. I told him of my fears and he listened patiently. I was afraid of leaving home and going to live with a man I barely knew. Joseph's practice was still unsettled. I was used to having anything my heart desired. What a materialistic young woman I was!"

Christine refilled the coffee cups and Grandma Em went on. "After I told Joseph of my fears, he just stood and looked at me for some minutes. When he spoke, Christine, his voice was quiet and deep, his heart in his eyes. 'I don't know what tomorrow holds, Emily, or if I'll be able to give you all the things your parents have. But I promise you, there won't be a day that goes by that you won't know, beyond a shadow of a doubt, that I love you with all my heart.'"

With this Grandma Em had both her and Christine in tears. "Don't, Christine, don't be afraid to talk with Luke. He is very understanding, and if you ever want to share your doubts, I promise he will listen."

Christine thanked Grandma Em for her words and the women continued to talk. By the time Silas and Luke returned, Christine was at ease again.

Within the hour Luke drove the women back to Grandma Em's. He stayed for a spell to get warmed up before heading back home.

Christine and Luke had a few minutes alone before he left.

"Thank you, Luke. It was a wonderful day."

"It was, wasn't it? The only thing missing was a good snowstorm that would have stranded you at the ranch a bit longer."

"Will I see you tomorrow?"

"I doubt it. Knowing that makes Sunday feel a week away." They stood in silence for a few minutes.

"I love you, Luke," Christine said, her eyes shimmering with unshed tears.

"Christie, why are you crying?"

Christine didn't know and could only give a small shrug. Luke was understanding and didn't push for an explanation. He simply drew her against him and held her, his cheek resting atop her head.

Much too soon he stepped back. "I have to go."

Christine tried to smile. "I'll see you Sunday."

"You'd think the way we're acting, it was going to be a year."

This did bring a smile to Christine's face, and in an instant Luke's lips were on her own. With his lips still touching hers he said, "Good night, Christie," and was gone.

47

"Good morning, Mrs. Hall. I hope I'm not calling too early."

"No, Sheriff, please come in."

"Is there someplace where we can talk?"

Mrs. Hall led the way into Joshua Bennett's study. She offered the sheriff some refreshment, but he declined.

"We found Carl Maxwell's body. He drowned."

Mrs. Hall's hand flew to her mouth and she gasped in horror.

"From the condition of the body, my guess is it was some time ago. There's no way for us to tell if it was an accident or deliberate."

"You mean suicide?" Mrs. Hall asked unbelievingly.

"No. I mean murder." Mrs. Hall sat heavily into a chair. The sheriff stood over her. He hated to upset her, but she was his link to the Bennett family and he needed her.

"Are you all right?"

Mrs. Hall fanned herself with her handkerchief. "Yes, Sheriff, I'm okay. I just wasn't expecting any news of this sort."

"I can assure you, Mrs. Hall, if there were any other way to handle this, I would."

"Of course, Sheriff." Mrs. Hall breathed deeply to compose herself. "What can I do to help?"

"Have you found anything in your search here in the study?"

"No, I've been through hundreds of papers but nothing that appears to be of utmost importance. I wish Christine were here." Mrs. Hall shot up out of the chair. "Christine! If Carl Maxwell was possibly murdered, they might be after Christine!"

"That's the next thing I needed to discuss with you." The sheriff summarized what the sheriff from Baxter had written. By the time he got to the burned man at the hotel, he was sure Mrs. Hall was going to faint.

But to his surprise she was made of tougher stuff than that. She composed herself after some minutes.

"I must admit to you, Sheriff, I have been most ignorant of how serious all this has become."

"And I'm sorry to upset you, but you can see why I need your help. I've been to see Vince Jeffers twice, and he nearly slams the door in my face over a few simple questions."

"Mr. Jeffers is not an easy man. There is something about him I can't quite place." Mrs. Hall shrugged.

"Will you write Miss Bennett about Carl Maxwell?"

"I hate to, but I really must. She needs to be on her guard. Her letters are very cheerful and I hate to put a damper on her happiness, but she must know."

"Please tell her to be careful and that I'm continuing my investigation here."

Mrs. Hall went then to prepare a light tea and handed the sheriff a few papers she had put aside. There was nothing pertinent, and as he left he encouraged her to keep searching.

48

"Oh no!"

"Bad news?"

"Yes, it's from Paul. He's not coming home for Christmas."

"Does he say why?"

"Oh, let me see." Grandma Em looked back at the letter in her hand. "It says here he'll be helping in a small church whose pastor was suddenly taken ill. He says 'As much as I want to be with you right now, these people need a pastor at Christmastime.' " Grandma Em stopped and blew her nose. "It just won't be the same without him."

Christine didn't know what to say. She knew the entire family would be sorely disappointed, since it was already December 12 and Christmas was less than two weeks away. It was too late to send Paul's gifts along to him.

"On Christmas morning we'll set aside all of Paul's gifts to box up and send to the school. They'll be waiting for him when he returns."

"That's a good idea! Thank you, Christine." Grandma Em was beginning to look happier.

Christine sensed that Grandma Em wanted to be alone, so she bundled up for a trip back downtown.

"But you just went," Grandma Em said in surprise.

"Yes, but there are a few things I forgot." Christine smiled and went out the door.

Baxter's general store was small but packed to the hilt with barrels of molasses, kerosene lamps, sacks of flour, a shiny new plow, and bolts of fabric. Christine could have looked all day.

She picked out the buttons she needed to finish Luke's Christmas present and then found two beautiful ribbons for Emily. She picked up extra yarn to finish the mittens for Calvin and Charles.

Christine took a few minutes after paying for her purchases to count out her money, and decided to pay some more on her medical bill.

The walk to Mark's place was cold, and Christine kept her head down against the wind. Had she been looking up, she would have seen a familiar horse out front.

"Well, Christine! What are you doing out on such a cold day?" Mark spoke and stepped to take her coat.

"Oh, I'm not staying. I just came to pay on my bill. Please, Mark, please let me pay without a lecture this time."

Mark agreed, but Christine could see he was not happy about it. He was still standing by the front door after Christine left when he heard Luke's footsteps on the hardwood steps.

Luke looked at the money in Mark's hand before turning questioning eyes to his brother.

"Don't say it, Luke. I've tried to talk with her, but you've got one independent woman on your hands.

Luke certainly couldn't argue with that. His hand went to his back pocket. He handed some bills to Mark. "If this doesn't cover it, let me know. If it's too much, put the balance in Christine's bank account." Luke reached for his coat and hat.

"Are you going to tell her?"

"Right now. If the next time you see me I have a few battle scars, you'll know why."

Christine had just taken off her things when Luke came in the front door.

"Hello!" he called out, and Christine came from the kitchen.

"Luke, I didn't know you were in town!"

"Actually, I was just at Mark's, but you left in such a hurry that you didn't see me."

"Oh, well, I just needed to pay on my bill and get home. It's too cold to be out."

Luke took Christine's hand and led her over to the couch.

"I talked to Mark after you left. I paid off your bill." Luke watched as a frown covered Christine's face.

"Why?" she asked flatly.

"Why what?"

"Don't mince words with me, Luke. I don't like to be a burden to anyone. You did not need to pay my bill."

"I realize I didn't need to pay your bill, but I wanted to. It was no burden. I had the money and it was my pleasure."

Christine couldn't come up with an argument after the simple, practical way he stated his case.

Luke watched as she stood and paced a bit before coming to stand before him.

"It just doesn't seem right."

"I love you, Christine, and I want to take care of you. What could be wrong with that?" Again she had no argument.

Christine stood for a moment in thought before bending and kissing Luke's cheek. "Thank you," she stated humbly, and Luke knew it had cost her. He was sure that in her own mind she was accepting a handout.

Before Luke could yield to the temptation of pulling her down into his lap he said, "Where's Gram?"

Christine sat beside him before she spoke. "I think she's upstairs. Your brother Paul wrote and he's not coming home for Christmas. I'm sorry, Luke."

Luke's face fell. "Our first Christmas without Paul! It won't be easy. I'll go up and see her."

Christine went into the kitchen to work on lunch. She prayed for Grandma Em and the family, asking God to give them a special peace about Paul's absence. She ended her prayer with a thankful heart that God had led her to a man as kind and sensitive as Luke Cameron.

49

"Hey, you're all bundled up! Don't tell me you're going somewhere. I just arrived."

"Luke, I got a letter from Spooner today. I need to go see Mark. Will you take me and then stay while we talk?"

Luke looked at Christine's face. She was pale and he could tell she had been crying. Wordlessly he led her to the cutter. Some of the snow had melted off and Christine wondered absently whether Christmas, only a few days away, would be a white one.

When Luke and Christine arrived, with Christine obviously upset, Maggie discreetly took the children and withdrew upstairs with them.

After the four adults were alone, Mark astutely guessed the problem. "You've heard from Spooner."

Christine nodded. "Mrs. Hall's letter came today. Carl Maxwell is dead. Mark, how could God let this happen? Carl was the only one who could answer my questions." Christine began to cry and Luke's arms went around her from his place next to her on the divan.

Sue's eyes also filled with tears and Mark reached for her hand.

"Christine," Mark said after she had composed herself, "what else did the letter say?"

Christine sniffed and pulled the letter from her skirt pocket. She handed it to Mark, who read it and then gave it to Luke.

"Listen, Christine, Mrs. Hall has not finished going through your grandfather's things yet. The sheriff is still on the job. And I think you've known deep in your heart for some time now that Carl Maxwell was probably dead. Am I right?"

Christine nodded.

Luke spoke up, correctly reading her mind. "Christine, none of this is your fault. I'm sure you feel helpless, but right now all that any of us can do is trust God to straighten this out."

Mark and Sue added their words of encouragement and Christine began to feel somewhat better. When Christine seemed in control again, Sue went to the kitchen to fix coffee. Mark went with her.

Once Luke and Christine were alone, Christine stood up and moved away from him. She didn't look at him when she spoke. "Everyone I get close to dies. If you don't want to see me anymore, Luke, I'll understand."

Luke was across the room in an instant and taking Christine's arms in his hands. Turning her around to face him, his words of rebuke at her foolish talk died in his throat at the misery he saw in her eyes. How could he explain to her that he was in over his head? If he told her about the burned man now, it would scare her witless. And the idea of no longer seeing her was like asking Luke Cameron to stop breathing.

"Christine, you haven't been listening to me. I love you. When a person loves someone, he doesn't run when he's needed the most. I'm going to be here beside you, taking care of you, loving you, and praying for you until you're sick of me."

"I will *never* be sick of you."

Susanne had started through the door back into the living room when she stopped so abruptly that Mark nearly ran into the back of her with the tray he was carrying.

Shifting to one side, Mark saw what had stopped his wife. In the front room stood Luke, holding in his arms the woman he loved. Knowing the way Christine was hurting, Mark and Sue wouldn't have interrupted them for anything, save another fire.

Mark put the tray back in the kitchen and leaned against the counter. "I think my brother had the right idea," Mark said as he pulled Sue against him. Sue looked up as she leaned against Mark's chest, her head not even up to her husband's chin.

"It's almost like watching *you* out there holding Christine."

Mark's eyebrows rose in surprise. "I can see, Mrs. Cameron, that if you've had time for such wild ideas, I've been neglecting you. I will remedy that instantly."

Susanne giggled and raised her mouth for his kiss.

The Cameron twins' thoughts at that moment were running on identical tracks: Home is anywhere as long as this woman is in my arms.

50

Christmas Eve Day. Christine lay in bed and stared up at the ceiling. If she were in Spooner right now and her grandfather were alive, they would be getting ready to go uptown for their traditional birthday breakfast. They had missed only one year since Christine was seven. The year she had turned 12 there was a blizzard, and Grandfather didn't want to risk getting caught in it.

Twenty years old! "Thank You, Lord," Christine prayed, "for finding me now when I still have most of my life to live with You in my heart." At the thought that her life might be cut short by a selfish man's greed, Christine pushed out of bed and refused to dwell on the idea.

Christine found Grandma Em up and breakfast ready. Grandma Em hugged Christine in the doorway. "Happy birthday, Christine!" Christine was surprised, since the only person she had told was Luke.

Grandma Em led her to the table. Christine was speechless as she sat down at her place to find a small, brightly wrapped package.

"I don't know what to say."

"Don't say anything. Just open it."

Under the wrapping Christine found a small black-bound diary.

"I know you came from Spooner without your things. The new year is upon us, and with all the changes you've been through, I thought you might find this helpful. Recording answers to prayer and then looking back on them can really lift your spirits."

Christine was too moved to speak. She turned the pages to see that Grandma Em had written in the front, "Happy 20th Birthday, Christine. May God bless you today and always. Love, Grandma Em. Proverbs 3:5,6."

Moving around the table, Christine kissed Grandma Em's cheek and hugged her. "Thank you," she said softly.

"You're welcome." Grandma Em smiled at her. "We've got a full day ahead of us. Let's eat."

Grandma Em was not kidding about the schedule. Silas would be bringing a tree in this afternoon and the parlor needed to be readied. At 6:00 there was to be a Christmas Eve service at church, and then the Cameron family would be headed back to trim Grandma Em's tree and have cookies with hot apple cider.

The day rushed by in a flurry of activity. Christine took a bath and dressed for the evening with special care. The dress she had made for the season was a deep green, near the color of her eyes. It had a high neck with long sleeves and a stark white collar and cuffs. Christine's hair, freshly washed, was brushed out and left long down her back.

The women were ready to go when Luke and Silas arrived to collect them. Christine was surprised but not disappointed when she saw Silas lead Grandma Em to a larger sleigh, one she had never seen before, while Luke guided her to the cutter and bundled her inside. The night air was crisp and Christine snuggled close to Luke.

The service that evening was one that Christine would never forget. The lamps were low, Pastor Nolan explained, because he didn't want the people to follow along in their Bibles but to just listen as he read.

"Luke 2. And it came to pass in those days that there went out a decree from Caesar Augustus that all the world should be taxed. (And this taxing was first made when Cyrenius was governor of Syria.) And all went to be taxed, everyone into his own city. And Joseph also went up from Galilee, out of the city of Nazareth, into Judaea, unto the city of David, which is called Bethlehem (because he was of the house and lineage of David), to be taxed with Mary, his espoused wife, being great with child. And so it was that, while they were there, the days were accomplished that she should be delivered. And she brought forth her first-born son, and wrapped him in swaddling clothes, and laid him in a manger, because there was no room for them in the inn. And there were in the same country shepherds abiding in the field, keeping watch over their flock by night. And, lo, the angel of the Lord came upon them, and the glory of the Lord shone round about them, and they were sore afraid. And the angel said unto them, 'Fear not, for behold, I bring you good tidings of great joy, which shall be to all people. For unto you is born this day in the city of David a Saviour, who is Christ the Lord. And this shall be a sign unto you: Ye shall find the babe wrapped in swaddling clothes, lying in a manger.' And suddenly there was with the angel a multitude of the heavenly host, praising God and saying, 'Glory to God in the highest, and on earth peace, good will toward men.' And it came to pass, as the angels were gone away from them into heaven, that the shepherds said to one another, 'Let us now go even unto Bethlehem, and see this thing which is come to pass, which the Lord hath made known unto us.' And they came with haste, and found Mary and Joseph and the babe lying in a manger. And when they had seen it, they made known abroad the saying which was told them concerning this child. And all they that heard it wondered at those things which were told them by the shepherds. But Mary kept all these things and pondered them in her heart. And the shepherds returned, glorifying and praising God for all the things that they had heard and seen, as it was told unto them."

Christmas took on a new meaning for Christine that night. She sat in awe as she thought of God coming to earth in the form of a tiny infant to one day become the Savior of her soul.

No hymnbook was opened and no music was played, but the congregation raised their voices in one accord. They sang with reverence and thanksgiving in their hearts.

Christine cried through most of the service and had to ask Luke for his handkerchief. When Pastor Nolan ended the service, Luke bent to tell Christine he had offered to douse the lamps and close up.

There were many hugs and much laughter. And when the last person left, Christine went to the stove for warmth as she waited for Luke to finish.

When the only light was a lamp burning up front and the fire, Luke joined Christine by the stove.

"Oh, Luke, it was such a beautiful service!"

He smiled tenderly.

"It makes such a difference hearing the story of Christ's birth when that same Christ lives within you."

They stood quietly together, unsure if the warmth they felt came from the fire without or within.

Luke reached into his pocket and brought out a thin gold chain. He held it for Christine's inspection. Hanging from the chain was a delicate gold locket, in the middle of which was a tiny diamond.

Luke waited until her eyes raised to his. "Happy birthday, Christine."

Christine struggled desperately to keep from crying and ruining this precious moment. Luke moved behind her and, raising his arms, clasped the necklace on her.

When Christine felt the locket drop below her throat, her finger reached for it and she gently opened it up to reveal an empty space within. Her eyes went questioningly to Luke.

"I was hoping you would put our picture inside, Christine—our wedding picture."

Christine's breath caught in her throat. She could only stare at the man before her.

"I wanted to ask you here, Christine, in church so you would know I've prayed and trusted God in this. Christine, will you marry me?"

"Oh, yes, Luke!" Christine spoke without hesitation and went into his arms. Luke held her as if he would never let her go, and Christine clung to him.

"When, Christine, when will you marry me?"

"Anytime you want." Christine was in a daze.

"January."

"But that's next month!" she answered, some sanity returning.

"January 21st. That's four weeks from today."

It was on the tip of her tongue to tell him it was too soon, but she looked into his eyes and knew she wanted it as well.

Without a word Christine nodded her head and Luke kissed her with all the love and longing he felt. In that kiss Christine knew it would be the same for her as it had been for Grandma Em. Every day she would awake and know that Luke Cameron loved her with all his heart.

51

January 5, 1888

My Dear Christie,

My heart is filled with joy over your wedding plans. I wish I could be there, and you know I would be if it were at all possible.

I continue on here, as I hope is your want. The house is in fine order and the horses are well taken care of. The sheriff spoke to the bank as you requested, and extra money was made available for salaries and household needs.

I hope this finds you safe. Please write and tell me about the wedding.

Love,

Mrs. Hall

"Her letter is a little shorter than usual and she didn't say anything about my accepting Christ," Christine commented to Luke as they sat at Grandma Em's kitchen table.

"Maybe she's afraid it will change things and she'll be out of a job."

"I've been thinking about that. I will have to go back home at some point. Things aren't really settled with grandfather's estate."

"When are you going to start thinking of Baxter as home?"

Christine could only stare at Luke, unsure of what he meant. Luke tugged on a strand of her hair. "I was just teasing, Christine. I didn't mean to upset you."

"There are times I don't know where home is, Luke. Can you understand that?"

"Considering what the last year of your life has been like, it's completely natural." He stood up. "I've got to go. As usual, I told Si I wouldn't be long, and then I stop over here and you won't let me leave."

"Oh no you don't, Luke Andrew Cameron! You're not going to blame your tardiness on me!" Christine shook her finger at him.

"You, Madam," Luke said with mock sternness, "are entirely too big for your britches and much too sassy. That is all going to change after we're married. Is that understood?"

"Yes, Luke," Christine answered with all the meekness she could muster.

"All right. Now act like a good wife and get my coat and hat." Christine moved like a humble servant and barely kept a straight face. While Luke was putting his coat and hat on, Christine moved around the kitchen table away from him.

"All right, I'm ready to go. You may come and kiss me goodbye."

"No."

Luke regarded his playfully defiant fiancée from across the table.

"Come here, Christie." His voice was no longer commanding but deep and persuasive.

Christine shook her head and stepped away from him as he moved toward her. His use of her nickname told her she would be kissed or he wouldn't be leaving.

"Come here, Christie, come and kiss me."

"You'd better kiss him, Christine, or Silas is going to end up feeding all those horses by himself." Grandma Em spoke matter-of-factly as she brought up jars of fruit from the basement.

Luke looked barely patient at the interruption but Christine was highly amused. She sauntered out from the kitchen to the parlor. "I'll walk you to the door." Her eyes told Luke she felt victorious.

"Bye, Gram."

"Bye, Luke."

"You think you're pretty clever, don't you?" They were at the front door and Luke was buttoning his coat.

"Pretty and clever, both," was Christine's sassy reply.

Luke threw back his head and roared with laughter. Christine never failed to delight him. Long after he kissed her goodbye and headed home, he was still laughing.

52

"Do you have the ring?"

"Yes, Luke. For the third time, I have the ring." Silas was calm as always, a steady rock in the storm.

"Did Julia get all of Christine's things moved in?"

"Last night. Christine will bring the last of her things after the ceremony."

"Does the house look okay?"

"It looks fine."

"Listen, Si. I've been thinking, and I just don't feel good about you staying with Grandma Em. This is your home. I don't want to do anything that will make you feel unwelcome. I know Christine feels the same . . ."

"Luke!" Silas' raised voice stopped Luke's tirade. He never shouted and Luke stood speechless.

"I do not feel that you and Christine are kicking me out of the house. It was my idea and it will only be for two nights. I'll be back Monday. Luke, you are bringing your bride home tonight and it's her I'm thinking of. The two of you need time alone together, if only for a few days, to start off your marriage on the right foot." Silas' voice was more firm than Luke had ever heard it.

Luke was grateful for Silas' words and nodded his agreement.

"Besides," Silas spoke as they headed out of the house, "you're only going to have her until Monday. Come Tuesday morning, she'll get one look at my hairy face and go screaming from the house." The men laughed at the long-standing joke and the tension evaporated.

The 2:00 sun was shining brightly overhead as Silas mounted his horse and Luke climbed into the cutter. They had a wedding to attend.

— ❖ —

"How does it look?"

"You look beautiful," Julia said earnestly.

"I look ten feet tall in all white," Christine replied with dismay. Julia and Susanne dissolved into giggles; both women agreed they had never seen a more radiant bride.

The women were in Grandma Em's room, and with less than an hour to the 3:00 o'clock ceremony Christine looked about to come unglued.

"She needs to see Luke," Julia said softly.

"I need my grandfather." Tears filled Christine's eyes as she spoke. "He should be here, to give me away. And Paul— Paul wasn't able to come, and that's not right." She was becoming frantic.

Christine did not notice Sue leave the room. But she was back momentarily, and with Grandma Em. She and Julia left them alone.

Upon seeing Grandma Em, Christine burst into tears. Grandma Em, drawing wisdom from every one of her 70 years, said nothing—not a word about teardrops on her wedding dress or how close it was to 3:00.

She knew Christine had slept poorly last night and had eaten nothing today. She also remembered how her own father had been too ill to walk her down the aisle and how devastated she had felt over this.

"I don't know what's wrong with me," Christine finally choked out. "I love Luke and I want to marry him. I just don't know what's wrong."

Grandma Em gently pulled Christine to the desk chair. She then moved the rocker close and began to pray. "Dear Father, help Christine. Please draw her near to Your throne, where she can find comfort and rest for emotions she herself may not even understand. You know of the love she and Luke have for each other. Calm her nerves and give her a peaceful heart to go down and marry the man she loves. If, Lord, there has been blindness, and Luke and Christine are not to be wed, please put Your hand down and prevent this marriage. Speak to Christine's heart so she will know Your will. We give this day and its glory to You. Amen."

Grandma Em sat quietly as Christine dried her face. "Would you like me to go get Luke? You know he'll come in an instant if you ask him."

Christine looked at the clock. 3:10. "Do you think he's upset with me?"

"No. Probably worried, but not upset."

Christine took a deep breath. "Will you please send Silas up in about five minutes?"

"I most certainly will. Do you want help with anything? Maybe Julia should come back up."

"No, I'll be fine. Thanks, Gram." Grandma Em didn't miss the use of the nickname that her grandchildren used. She hugged Christine and nearly glowed with happiness as she left the room.

Christine stepped before the full-length mirror. Her hair was still in place, swept up in curls atop her head.

Her dress was snow-white satin. The skirt was full and gathered at the waist. Puffed sleeves at the shoulder fit snugly along Christine's arms and buttoned tightly at the wrist. The satin on the bodice was overlayed with hand-made lace that ran in a V from the nipped-in waist to a high, stand-up collar. The same pearl buttons that buttoned at the wrist ran full length down Christine's back.

Luke loved Christine's hair and had asked her not to cover it. Christine was taking a close-up check for signs of tears when Silas knocked.

Silas kissed her cheek before offering his left arm. They paused at the top of the stairs. "Are you okay?"

Christine nodded. "Thanks, Si."

Luke stood in the parlor awaiting his bride. The urge to go to her had been nearly overpowering, but Grandma Em had told him that all was fine and that Christine would be down in about five minutes. He didn't care that the ceremony hadn't started on time or that the kids were getting squirmy; he just wanted to see Christine and know she was all right.

The relief he felt upon hearing the rustle of her dress on the stairs just before she came into view was poignantly sweet.

Nothing could have prepared Luke for the vision of Christine in her wedding dress. He could only stare. Christine's eyes searched his out and the rest of the room faded from view.

Christine remembered little of the ceremony. She would always cherish Luke's eyes as he said "I do," the pressure of his hand holding hers, watching his hand slip the ring onto her finger, and their first kiss as man and wife, tender and warm.

Mark and Julia had stood up with them. Pastor Nolan performed the ceremony while Mrs. Nolan played the piano. The parlor was filled with family and friends from church.

The reception was well under way. Gram, Julia, and Sue had prepared a feast. When Luke and Christine were finally seated, their plates full, Luke asked, "Are you okay?"

"Just an attack of nerves. Are you angry?"

"Furious," Luke stated with a smile.

The time flew by, and before long everyone was at the front door waving and shouting blessings and good wishes to the newlyweds as the cutter bore them away.

The horse's fast pace and the gusty wind made conversation nearly impossible. Christine was starting to feel chilled as they reached the house.

Christine was picked up and carried into the front room of the ranch house, then set down and a lamp lit before either person uttered a word.

"Welcome home, Mrs. Cameron."

Christine's face glowed with happiness. "I like the sound of that."

Luke handed Christine the lamp. "Go get warmed up while I take care of the horse."

Christine stood still a few moments after the door closed behind Luke, smiling at her surroundings.

With the lamp in one hand and a small suitcase in the other, Christine headed toward the hallway that led off the dining area.

Luke's room, and now hers, was halfway down the hall and at the back of the house. It was a huge room with a massive four-poster bed, a matched set of wardrobes, and the largest bureau that Christine had ever seen. In one corner, having been stoked that afternoon, burned a wood stove, making the room comfortably warm.

Julia had shown Christine through the bedrooms the week before. She ran her hand over the beautiful quilt on the bed. Luke's mother had made it—a mother-in-law that Christine would not know personally, but only through Luke's words and her handiwork here and there in the house.

Christine opened the wardrobe door. Seeing her things hanging beside Luke's gave her a feeling of contentment. She heard a door close and knew that Luke was back.

Luke followed the light from Christine's lamp and found her in his bedroom, *their* bedroom. Upon entering, Luke closed the door and leaned against it.

Christine was still in her wedding dress, her hair coming loose around her face. Luke was in his dark suit and crisp white shirt, so tall and handsome. Husband and wife stood in silence regarding each other. Luke spoke from his place at the door.

"Christine, it's been a long day. I know you're tired, and if you'd rather..." Luke halted as Christine moved toward him, her heart swelling with love at how thoughtful he was of her well-being.

When she stood directly in front of him, all she could think to say was, "I love you, Luke."

Luke understood and drew Christine to him, hardly able to believe that a man could be so happy and blessed.

Theirs was a love sprung deep from within, willing and able to stand the test of time, come what may, with Christ at the head of their home.

53

Never would Luke or Silas have believed they could be so spoiled so quickly: baked goods in abundance, hot meals served, coffee always waiting on the stove, the house spotless, and clothes always clean—all brought on by Christine's presence.

Christine was a morning person, and Luke's only complaint was that the warm person beside him all night was not there most mornings when he awoke. But the warm kitchen and hot coffee could not be faulted.

For nearly two weeks Christine laughed at the sight of her new brother-in-law first thing in the morning. Silas would try to act as grumpy as he looked, but Christine only laughed harder and he gave up.

Every Thursday Christine spent the day at Grandma Em's. Christine insisted upon coming back once a week to help out. There had been a battle, but Christine won.

"You'd think I was 100 years old the way you're acting."

"I do not think you are 100 years old. I know very well you'll be 71 next month, but that's beside the point."

"But, Christine, you have your own house to take care of now!" Grandma Em said as she tried a new approach.

"My house is not going to suffer the one day I come to see you. Now, what day shall we make it?" Grandma Em was stubbornly silent.

"All right! I'll pick a day myself. Thursday. I'll be here Thursday morning at 8:00."

"Less than a month you've been married, and she sounds just like you," Grandma Em said accusingly to Luke, who was sitting quietly on the couch, watching his wife in battle.

Luke opened his mouth to defend himself, but Christine broke in. "Luke has nothing to do with this. It was my idea, and I will not change my mind."

Grandma Em could see she was not going to win this battle, but she was not about to give in gracefully. "Is your salary to be the same as before?" Grandma Em asked innocently.

Christine was out of her chair in a flash and standing, arms akimbo before her husband. "Talk to her! Tell your grandmother I *will* be here on Thursdays to give her a hand and if she gives me one cent, I'll burn it!" This said, Christine stomped into the kitchen. Luke and Grandma Em listened a minute as she banged and slammed around preparing some coffee.

"How do you really feel about Christine coming?"

"I'm delighted to have her."

"That's what I thought," Luke said, his eyes twinkling. "You really shouldn't have teased her. You got me in trouble."

"That was the best part!" Grandma Em replied as she headed to the kitchen to make her peace with Christine.

54

Using the back of her hand, Mrs. Hall brushed a fallen strand of hair from her face. Her eyes fell on a small slip of paper sticking out of a stack she was reading through. 284539. She contemplated the odd set of numbers for a time before setting the paper aside.

Sunday was no time to be going through the study at the Bennett residence, but she was drawing close to the end and was anxious to be done. Her fingers went to her temples and she rubbed gently. 284539. What an odd combination of numbers. Combination! The safe! Mrs. Hall reached quickly for the paper. She had nearly forgotten the safe.

Mrs. Hall went to a small wood cabinet that sat inconspicuously behind the desk below the two windows. The door opened easily to reveal the black safe within.

Mrs. Hall looked again at the numbers in her hand and then knelt on the floor. The first two tries with the dial were unsuccessful, but on the third attempt she heard a click. Reaching carefully for the handle, she turned it and pulled.

Her heart was pounding as she swung the door open. She rose quickly and moved the desk lamp close. A musty smell hit her nose when she resumed her place on the floor.

For a moment she touched nothing, but she held the lamp high and peered within the small cavern of the safe. A large, yellowish bundle of papers caught her eye and she reached for it.

Mrs. Hall recognized Joshua Bennett's own handwriting on the first page. It took the weary housekeeper some minutes to realize she was reading a will—Joshua Bennett's last will and testament written in his own hand.

With sudden clarity Mrs. Hall was transported back through time: "...she will receive the house and stables along with the rest of my holdings. In the event of her death, the inheritance will go to my partner, Vince Jeffers." Carl Maxwell had read those words in a quiet, almost apologetic voice.

What a blind fool she had been! To be sure of her theory, she quickly scanned the pages in her hand. There was not a word about Vince Jeffers. Nearly everything was left unconditionally to Christine.

Mrs. Hall struggled up from her cramped position on the floor. Donning her coat and hat, she quickly grabbed up the incriminating papers and rushed for the front door.

— ✜ —

"I think we should eat at 7:00. How is that for your families?"

"Sounds fine," Julia answered.

"No problem that I can think of," Susanne said, then added, "Pending as always Mark's work. We'll just bring Grandma Em with us."

"Julia, are you going to do the pies?" Christine asked.

"I'd planned on it. I put up jars and jars of peaches, and that's her favorite."

"Okay, Sue's doing a chocolate cake and I'm covering supper, so I think we're all set." Christine would have said more, but the moment Grandma entered the kitchen, the three women stopped talking.

When the silence lengthened through Grandma Em washing a spot on her dress, she became suspicious. "Why do I get the distinct feeling I was being discussed?" Grandma Em asked while approaching the table.

The women knew she had to be told, but they hated to spoil her Sunday. In their hesitation, she figured it out for herself.

"Oh, you girls! You're planning something for Friday, aren't you? I told you last year there would be no more parties, but you didn't listen. You need to be spanked and I'm going to go get your husbands."

Christine looked a bit thunderstruck, but Julia and Susanne had heard all this before.

Within minutes Mac, Luke, and Mark entered the kitchen. Julia stood and gave Mac her chair. As she expected, she was pulled down into his lap as soon as he was settled. Mark stood behind Susanne, his hands resting on her shoulders. Luke took the chair next to Christine after moving it close beside hers.

"Where are the children?" Sue asked. "Emily is out for the count on the sofa and the boys went out to play with Silas," her husband answered.

"And Gram?"

"She headed upstairs after telling us you three were in plot against her."

"You must have been discussing Friday," Luke guessed, since he and Christine had already talked it over.

"Is it true she says no more parties every year?" Christine wanted to know.

"Just about, but she loves them and always has more fun than anyone else."

"By March, when the cold weather feels like it's never going to end, everyone is in need of a party."

The six adults talked around the table for awhile. When Christine heard one of the boys run by outside and Silas call to him, she commented absently and to no one in particular, "I wish Silas were in here with his wife."

It was a subject that had crossed everyone's mind at one time or another.

"Has Si said anything to you, Christine? About wanting a wife, I mean?"

"No, not directly, or even indirectly, for that matter. It's just that at times he looks a bit lost and lonely. I didn't mean to make you cry, Julia." Christine felt bad.

Julia shook her head in mute apology over the display of tears and Mac said, "It's not your fault, Christine. Some people are born with an overabundance of tears. Julia has enough for six people." Everyone laughed at this, and the spell was broken.

They continued to talk and make plans until Elizabeth began to complain about an empty stomach from the cradle in the parlor.

Soon everyone broke up to return to their own homes, the prospect of a party on Friday buoying everyone's mood.

— ❖ —

"I need to see Mr. Jeffers." The sheriff in Spooner spoke as soon as the housekeeper allowed him into the entryway.

"I'm terribly sorry, but he's not home. Perhaps you'd like to leave a message."

"When will he be back? It's urgent."

The housekeeper hesitated.

"I repeat, it is urgent that I speak with him."

"He's not here and I don't know where he is. When I arrived this morning, there was only a note saying he would be away and to keep the house in order." The servant looked frightened.

"Let me see the note." The sheriff's voice was abrupt in his agitated state over Vince Jeffers getting away. The housekeeper scurried to comply with the order.

Upon reading it and taking a quick look around, the sheriff's hopes plummeted. From all appearances, Vince Jeffers had disappeared without a trace.

55

Luke rolled and stretched, his body protesting the idea of getting out of bed. When something tickled his nose, Luke reached up and pulled away a stray hair. He smiled as it just kept coming. He wound the strand from Christine's head around his finger.

It was time, he knew—time to come clean and confess to Christine what he had been holding back. He had been feeling the pain of disobedience in his heart long enough. It was time to talk with his wife and to trust God.

"Oh, Luke, I thought you would be up! I really need to make that bed. I have so much to get done before the party." Christine spoke as she bustled around the room.

The party for Grandma Em. Luke had forgotten all about it. "Tomorrow, Lord," Luke promised; "tomorrow I'll tell her."

"Luke Cameron, are you going to get out of that bed today?" Christine stood at the foot, her brows raised in question.

"You could come over and help me up." Luke's voice was gravelly with sleep.

"Do I have your word that you will come out and I won't get pulled in?" At Luke's silence, Christine laughed. "I thought not." With a flick of her wrist Christine threw back the covers, causing Luke to shiver and leap for the stove.

"You're a cruel woman," he grumbled as he dressed quickly. But Christine had the bed half made and just ignored him.

When the men came back in from the horses, Christine asked about the road. "I really need to get to town. The storm this week has put me behind schedule. I didn't even get to Grandma Em's this week."

Silas answered her. "I've got to go in this afternoon. You can go with me."

"That's fine, Si, thanks. I can have supper almost ready before we go."

It crossed Luke's mind to tell Christine he would rather she stay inside today. Knowing she would ask why and that he had no reason, he held his tongue.

— ✦ —

"You're sure?"

"Yes, I'm sure. I'll go straight over as soon as I'm done here and ride with them. You go back and I'll see you tonight."

"Okay, but you be careful."

"I'll be fine. Thanks for the ride, Silas."

Christine turned away, but Silas still hesitated at the door of the general store. His business in town had been brief, and he had heard from some buyers and wanted to get home to tell Luke. Christine was to go to Mark and Sue's for a ride home. Silas went ahead out to the sleigh. Christine was a big girl and she would make the two blocks safely.

— ✦ —

"Is it almost time?" Emily danced around her mother's legs.

"Almost. I've got to wrap up this cake and bundle up your sister. Don't forget, we have to pick up Grandma Em too."

"Won't Aunt Christine be surprised that we're coming early to help?"

"I'm sure she will. Now don't forget to say happy birthday to Grandma Em when we see her, and don't tell her what's in the box we wrapped."

"I won't. Is it time to tell Daddy we're ready?"

"Yes, you go ahead and tell him about 15 minutes."

Emily, always happy to be of help, skipped off toward her father's office.

— ✦ —

"Red or blue," Christine said under her breath. She

needed calico for the border of her new quilt and could go with either color.

"Ma'am." A voice broke through her thoughts.

Christine looked down at the small child standing beside her. She did not remember seeing this child before. Wordlessly, Christine was handed a note and the child ran from the store. She stared after him in some surprise before reading the paper in her hand.

"Christine," it read, "come immediately to the house. Grandma Em has been hurt."

The note was unsigned, but Christine was sure it was from Mark. The snow was deep and it hindered Christine's progress as she rushed with a fearful heart. Of all things! Grandma Em injured on her 71st birthday!

Christine quickly climbed the front porch steps and rushed in the front door.

"Gram!" Christine called as she quickly unbuttoned her coat and moved into the parlor.

"By all means, Christine, take off your coat. You're going to be here awhile."

Christine's movements stilled and she felt her blood run cold. Until that moment she believed she would never hear the voice of Vince Jeffers again.

He was seated on the sofa. Resting beside him on the seat and close on his right was a long, wicked-looking knife.

"Take off your coat, Christine." This time it was an order, and Christine obeyed. She laid the coat over the nearest chair and looked up to see Vince's eyes moving over her. A leering smile played across his lips and Christine felt dirty beneath his perusal.

"Please, God," Christine thought, asking for she knew not what, just needing to cry out to her Savior.

"What are you doing here, Vince?" Christine was amazed at how calm her voice sounded.

"I'm surprised you have to ask that, Christine. You didn't actually think I was going to let you get away with all that money, did you?"

"What money?" Christine asked in genuine confusion.

Vince's scornful laugh grated on Christine's nerves. "You're as big a fool as your grandfather was," he snarled at her as he stood up.

Christine was still completely baffled, and Vince could see this. She watched, horrified, as the snarl on his face became almost a pleasant smile. This man was mad.

"The railroad stocks," he informed her, as if he were announcing the time of day.

"The railroad stocks? The ones you advised Grandfather to sell because they were worthless?"

"Yes, one and the same. He was a fool. He never even checked on my story—just handed me the papers so I could take care of it."

"But the stocks are worth something after all?" Christine asked, trying desperately to get some understanding of the situation while praying constantly for help, helpless as it was. No one knew that Vince Jeffers was here or that she was at Grandma Em's.

"Worth something?" Again that scornful laugh. "They're worth a small fortune, but I can't touch it. By the time I realized I needed your grandfather's signature, he was already dead."

"No, I didn't kill him," Vince assured her upon seeing the look on her face. "But it was very nice of him to die when he did. I really am in deep financial trouble, you know." He stated this so calmly that Christine felt her stomach lurch.

"Do I nauseate you, Christine?" Vince had not missed the look of revulsion on her face, and he approached slowly as he spoke. "That's really a shame, you know." He was almost next to her. "Because we're going to get to know one another very well." Christine had backed up flush against the wall and Vince stopped within inches of her. His hand came up to her face and Christine tried to turn into the wall. Vince fed on her fear, and his laugh was a low hiss as sour breath fell on her face. She felt his fingers at the side of her neck. "Yes, Christine, very well indeed."

— ⁜ —

"It's Mark," Silas said from his place at the window.

Luke felt relief wash over him. He had been anxious all day about Christine and couldn't wait to see her.

Grandma Em was the first one in the house. Silas and Luke both hugged her before she could get her coat off, wishing her birthday greetings. Not until Susanne and Emily were inside, and Mark, with the baby in his arms, began to shut the door did Luke ask.

"Where's Christine?" The room became completely still at his question.

"Isn't she here, Luke?" Mark asked.

Silas broke in. "She was supposed to come to your house after she was done in town and ride back here with you."

"We left a little early. Maybe she missed us," Grandma Em suggested.

"It wasn't that early," Mark said, his eyes locked with Luke's.

Luke felt as if the walls were closing in. The feeling of dread and worry that Christine was in trouble had been with him all day, and already it could be too late. He took control just as the MacDonalds walked in the door.

"Silas, take Mac's sleigh and ride for the sheriff. I'll go with Mark. Bring him as fast as you can to Grandma Em's. Mac, stay here. Sue can explain everything." In a flurry of grabbed coats and hats the three men were out the door.

Luke never would have believed the ride to town could take so long. Mark was whipping the horse into a near frenzy in order to gain speed, but the snow was deep and it seemed as though an eternity had passed.

As his stomach churned in fear, Luke allowed himself to imagine that Christine was all right. He pictured her shopping in the general store, ignorant of anyone intending to harm her.

But the image did not last. The sense of foreboding which had rode him hard throughout the day assured him—Christine was in danger. How could he possibly live with himself knowing his own sin had cost him the most precious person in his life.

"Please God," Luke prayed under his breath as both sleighs nearly flew into town, "please let us be on time."

— ⁘ —

"Take your shoes off!" Vince suddenly snapped into Christine's face. When Christine hesitated, again feeling a sickening horror at his change of moods, he picked up the knife. "I've always hated it that you were taller than me." Christine moved quickly to do as he bade. The low heeled boots made little difference, but he seemed pleased.

His eyes were undressing her again and Christine thought frantically on how to divert his attention.

"Vince, do you know anything about Carl Maxwell's death?"

"Don't mention that spineless fool to me." He waved the knife around as he spoke. "I needed a new partner to help me with a few things in your grandfather's estate, but he turned out to be a gutless idiot. Oh, he had no trouble drawing up that fake will, but he became quite squirmish when I said you had to die. He thought he was so clever, sending you to Fall Creek."

"Did you kill that man in Fall Creek?" Christine whispered.

"No, no, that was just a freak thing. It caused me a lot of trouble too—you running all the way down here. It took us forever to find you and then when we did, my man couldn't even burn a barn properly. Never send a boy to do a man's work." Vince sneered, his face an ugly scowling mask.

What little color was left in Christine's face drained away. The barn burning was attempted murder! "Oh, God," she prayed silently, "please help me!"

"How many people have you killed in your greed, Vince? What was in grandfather's will that you had to change? He was good and generous." Christine was crying now, not even sure of what she was saying, and it angered Vince.

"Stop your blubbering. Your grandfather was soft. Why, he left over a thousand dollars to that orphanage. What a waste! Carl Maxwell was soft too, and he got in my way." The sneer in Vince's voice softened as he approached Christine again. "And you're going to find out, Christine, when people get in my way, I must remove them."

He was in front of her again, the knife held straight at her. When she felt the tip of the knife move against a button on her blouse and heard it hit the floor, she prayed again. "Please God, please help me." Luke flashed through her mind.

"I'm through with the games now, Christine," Vince said in yet another tone of voice. "Take off the blouse."

"No, please, Vince," she whispered.

"Take it off!" he screamed at her, and Christine felt the knife prick her throat. Visions of another knife in an alley made Christine's hands shake so much she couldn't loosen the buttons.

With an angry curse, Vince reached to the neckline of the blouse and yanked. Christine's head was snapped forward and buttons flew everywhere.

Her hands came up to hold the gaping blouse together and she heard her name.

"Christine!"

Vince turned to the intruding voice and Christine saw Luke and the sheriff coming into the parlor from the kitchen.

Vince spun back quickly and raised the knife over Christine, but a shot rang out and Christine watched the knife fly from Vince's hand. At that same instant, he clutched his bleeding elbow and began to scream in agony.

Christine watched as the sheriff, with little regard for the screaming man's elbow, dragged him from the room. Christine could hear his hysterical tirade, shouting against her grandfather and her until the kitchen door slammed, and the room was covered with an almost eerie silence.

Unaware of any other presence in the room, Christine started when she felt gentle hands on her upper arms. Even upon seeing it was Luke, Christine could not stop herself from bolting away from his touch.

Luke felt a myriad of emotions flood through him as his wife recoiled from him and backed toward the stairs. Her eyes were wide with panic. Her blouse was ripped open and there was a cut bleeding on her neck. Luke felt sick with the knowledge that this was his fault.

He had thought if they could just be in time, everything would be fine, never once considering the shock his wife would be in. He knew in that instant if it took the rest of his life, he would put this behind them. He would be there for her so she would have nothing more to fear.

"Christine." Luke's voice was quiet, his eyes moist. At that soft familiar voice calling her name, Christine seemed to gain a bit of control.

"He ripped my blouse," she said, her voice like a lost little girl's, and Luke's heart broke.

Luke continued on in the same quiet voice, tenderness in every syllable as his heart overflowed with love for this woman.

"It's over now, Christie. He's gone. The sheriff has him and he can't hurt you anymore. It's my fault. I should have told you about the barn fire. I wanted so much to take care of you, and all I did was hurt you. I'm sorry." Luke's voice broke on these last words.

"I was so scared," Christine began to sob.

"It's over now," Luke still did not approach her for fear of frightening her more. With his arms outstretched he said, "Come to me, Christie. Come and let me hold you."

Luke waited until Christine took one step and then covered the distance between them and swept her into his arms. They clung together and cried. Tears of frustration, anger, fear, and relief. Tears of joy and thanksgiving. Holding tightly to each other, they cried tears that marked the end of a pain-filled season and the beginning of a time for healing.

Epilogue

May in Baxter meant sunshine, warm weather, flowers blooming and spring planting. Christine had begun to think it would never warm up, but May brought a warmth that let the grass grow tall and green.

Christine sat among the grass atop a small knoll thinking back over the past year and all its changes. Her mind went back to the night when a frightened 19-year-old woman had, in a boy's disguise, run from her home. Arriving in Baxter, meeting the Camerons, seeing her need for Christ and accepting Him. Her marriage to Luke and the awful confrontation with Vince Jeffers. A frown covered Christine's face. Vince and the man who had started the barn fire had been sent back to Spooner. They would both stand trial for their deeds.

Soon Luke and Christine would head to Spooner to clear up Joshua Bennett's estate. Christine would also have to testify against Vince Jeffers, a task she did not relish. She watched Luke come out of the house, and when he looked her way, she waved. She smiled when he started toward her.

Was it possible to be so in love? Every day was more precious than the last. Christine's hand went to her still-flat stomach. She would have to tell him her suspicions soon. She hesitated only because she wanted to be sure.

Upon spotting his wife sitting off by herself, Luke became alert. She had had another nightmare last night. They had decreased some, but as always, Luke was concerned for her. They both knew when it was time to return to Spooner, there would be memories to upset her. Luke was reluctant to do anything that would stir up the hurt, but they had little choice. Christine stood and they shared a sweet kiss before Luke asked, "Are you okay?"

"I'm fine," Christine assured him. "I was just thinking over the last year."

"It hasn't been an easy one. Are you thinking about going home?"

Christine smiled and shook her head at him. Luke, misinterpreting, was about to tell her they could possibly delay the trip if she was uneasy about it, but Christine spoke.

"Luke," Christine's voice was whisper soft, her eyes shining with love. "Home is here in Baxter with you. Our time in Spooner will be temporary. You are my home, and wherever God leads you, I'll be by your side, knowing we're within His will."

Luke smiled at her and spoke gently. "My precious Christine, I have prayed so long for that peace in your heart. I've known for some time that where you are is a place called home."